THE
DAY THE
MUSTACHE
TOOK OVER

Alan Katz

illustrations by Kris Easler

BLOOMSBURY

NEW YORK   LONDON   OXFORD   NEW DELHI   SYDNEY

With love to my sons, David and Nathan . . .

a truly one-of-a-kind twosome!

Text copyright © 2015 by Alan Katz
Illustrations copyright © 2015 by Kris Easler

First published in the United States of America in September 2015
by Bloomsbury Children's Books
Paperback edition published in October 2016
www.bloomsbury.com

Bloomsbury is a registered trademark of Bloomsbury Publishing Plc

For information about permission to reproduce selections from this book, write to
Permissions, Bloomsbury Children's Books, 1385 Broadway, New York, New York 10018
Bloomsbury books may be purchased for business or promotional use. For information on
bulk purchases please contact Macmillan Corporate and Premium Sales Department at
specialmarkets@macmillan.com

The Library of Congress has cataloged the hardcover edition as follows:
Katz, Alan.
The day the mustache took over / by Alan Katz; illustrated by Kris Easler.
pages   cm
Summary: David and Nathan are twin brothers who just can't seem to
keep a babysitter around for long—they've had 347 after all. Or is it 734?
Either way, there's got to be someone who can handle these two. Enter
Martin Healey Discount, or "Murray Poopins" as the boys dub him.
ISBN 978-1-61963-558-6 (hardcover) • ISBN 978-1-61963-559-3 (e-book)
[1. Babysitters—Fiction. 2. Behavior—Fiction. 3. Twins—Fiction. 4. Brothers—Fiction.
5. Humorous stories—Fiction.] I. Easler, Kris, illustrator. II. Title.
PZ7.K15669Day 2015   [Fic]—dc23   2014034289

ISBN 978-1-68119-148-5 (paperback)

Book design by Amanda Bartlett
Typeset by Integra Software Services Pvt. Ltd.
Printed and bound in the U.S.A. by Berryville Graphics Inc., Berryville, Virginia
2 4 6 8 10 9 7 5 3 1

THE DAY THE MUSTACHE TOOK OVER

Praise for

THE
DAY THE
MUSTACHE
TOOK OVER

"The humor in the book will certainly appeal to fans of Jeff Kinney's Diary of a Wimpy Kid and Lincoln Peirce's Big Nate, and Easler's illustrations add to the hilarity." —*School Library Journal*

"The twins are mischievous on their own, but Martin's arrival brings a previously unmatched level of absurdity that is sure to delight young readers. . . . This nonsensical, entertaining tale brings humor and fun to new heights." —*Publishers Weekly*

"The line drawings of innocent-looking lads and frazzled adults add further comical notes to this mischievous riff on the Travers classic." —*Booklist*

"Much random silliness and outlandish mischief will appeal to young readers. Simple language, readable sentences, and satisfyingly predictable twists offer an easy read for reluctant readers. Move over, Mary Poppins." —*School Library Connection*

Books by Alan Katz

The Day the Mustache Took Over
The Day the Mustache Came Back

CHAPTER
ONE

"Boys, boys, boys, boys, boys!" Josephine screamed at twin brothers Nathan and David Wohlfardt as they jumped from here to there and back to here in their family living room.

"Yes, yes, yes, yes, yes, yes?" David answered.

"That's one too many yeses," Nathan told him. "Our nanny Josephine yelled 'boys' five times, and you said 'yes' six times."

"No, no, no, no, no, no, no I didn't," David responded.

"Yes, yes, yes, yes, yes, yes, yes, yes you did," Nathan corrected.

"I don't think so," David said.

"I do think so," Nathan said.

"I beg to differ," David said.

"I dig to barfer," Nathan said.

"That doesn't even make sense," David said.

"I fiff to darber," Nathan said.

"BOYS!" Josephine shouted, stopping the twins in their tracks (and that isn't just an expression—Nathan and David were literally leaving muddy, cruddy tracks as they hopped, skipped, jumped, bumped, and ran themselves silly around the room).

Josephine continued, "I have been a caretaker for children of all ages, in homes all across this fine nation, but I have never, never, never—"

"That's three 'nevers' so far," David said.

"The ugly twin is correct," Nathan said. "For the first time ever, I might add."

"—never, never, *never* seen behavior so consistently improper. When it comes to disrespect, you boys take the cake!"

"There's cake?" David asked. "Yum."

"I'm not sure you're right, Josephine," Nathan told her as he pretended to grab a microphone and addressed a nonexistent camera.

"This is Nathan Wohlfardt, reporting for the Wohlfardt News Network. I'm standing in the Wohlfardt home at 82727294 Flerch Street in Screamersville, Virginia, and I'm here to cover the election to find the two nicest, kindest, most well-behaved kids in America. Young lady, what is your name and who gets your vote?"

"First of all," David said into the fake microphone, "I am *not* a young lady. My name is David Wohlfardt, and I vote for David Wohlfardt."

"Have you considered the other very fine candidate, Nathan Wohlfardt?" Nathan asked.

"Never heard of him," David said.

"Why, he's the extraordinarily wonderful young man who lets you share his bedroom and bathroom," Nathan told him.

"Well, I don't recognize the name, but the disgusting smell is familiar," David said.

"Nevertheless, let's tally the ballots. One ridiculous vote has been cast for David Wohlfardt, and there's one intelligent vote for Nathan Wohlfardt. It's official: the brothers are the two nicest, kindest, most well-behaved boys in America! This is Nathan Wohlfardt for the Wohlfardt News Network, signing off."

The boys waved their arms in mock celebration.

Nathan put down the fake microphone and said, "So you see, Josephine, when it comes to good behavior, we are . . ."

Josephine was nowhere in sight.

"Where'd she go?" Nathan wanted to know.

"I think *she* signed off too," David told him.

Indeed, the front door was open. Josephine's hat and coat were gone. And on the table near the door—right next to Nathan's muddy soccer cleats—was a handwritten note:

I quit for two reasons.
1. David
2. Nathan

"Another alphabetical quitter," David said as he put her resignation letter in the stack with the many, many, many others.

"Mom and Dad will be *so* pleased," Nathan added.

"NOT," they both said, agreeing for the first time since, well, since the nanny prior to Josephine had quit several weeks before.

CHAPTER TWO

In so many ways, Josephine (wherever she went) was right. The truth is, you'd never use the words "well" and "behaved" in the same sentence to describe Nathan and David *when they're together*. When his brother isn't around, Nathan can be polite, friendly, cute, charming, clever, and smart. The same can be said about David—when his twin is somewhere else.

But somehow they don't blend as a duo. Just like mixing oil and water, cats and dogs, or laundry detergent and cranberry juice, when the boys are together, there's disharmony. Friction. And trouble.

For example, Nathan loves vegetables (the fresher and crunchier, the better). David, on the other hand, hates, hates, *hates* anything green that's grown in the ground. Put some on his dinner plate and he'll howl and yelp but never gulp. However . . .

NATHAN

Put those same vegetables on his brother Nathan's plate, and David'll yell, "Hey, where's *mine*?" then grab them off Nathan's plate and gobble 'em down.

Here's another thing: David loves building things. Give him playing cards, blocks, shoe boxes, or pretty much anything he can stack, and within minutes, he'll erect a whole miniature town. It's pretty amazing.

What's also pretty amazing is Nathan's supersonic radar that tells him when David's finished building something. Without fail, that is exactly the moment Nathan shows up with an accidentally misthrown football to de-town the town.

DAVID

Need more proof? David sings. Nathan hates music and refuses to sing any-thing. Even "Happy Birth-day." Nathan swims. David's a dry-land kind of kid. David can watch a whole movie on TV from start to finish without getting up once. Nathan's never viewed anything for more than twenty-three seconds without clicking the remote 117 times.

And so on and so forth. As Nathan once said, "When it comes to the Wohlfardt boys, every day is opposite day." Naturally, David disagreed.

It's understandable, of course, that one of the boys (Nathan) is always on time and the other (David) is always late. Though they both do manage to get to school before the bell rings, which isn't really that hard because they live right next door to the school. They can stay in bed until 7:56 and still be in their classrooms by 8:00. Unless it's the day they both take showers. Then they have to get up at 7:55 instead.

And when it comes to neatness . . . well, don't ask. With all the junk in their room, it's hard to tell if there's a carpet on the floor. In fact, it's hard to tell if there *is* a floor. And forget about finding a trash can. In fact, the last thing Nathan threw away was . . . David.

Schoolwork? Let's put it this way: Last week, David finished all his first-grade math assignments in one afternoon. Which would be pretty good if he weren't already in third grade!

And, like most brothers, the boys fight. They argue. And they bicker.

In fact, they fight, argue, and bicker about everything. Recently they fought about whether they were arguing or bickering. This time it was over the schedule their parents made for them so they wouldn't fight about their chores.

Then what did they fight about?

"I get to look at the schedule first."

"No, I do!"

"No, I do!"

"No, I do!"

"No, you're after me!"

"No, you're after me!"

"I forgot what we're fighting about."

That's life with the Wohlfardt brothers. Some people have a talent for chasing butterflies. Some are great at chasing away the blues. Nathan and David, however, are world-class experts at chasing away . . .

CHAPTER
THREE

"NANNIES!" Mr. Wohlfardt bellowed. "Au pairs, live-in childcare givers, executive home-life leadership engineers—call them what you will they all mean 'babysitter,'" he continued. "And that's something we just can't seem to keep in this house!"

"Boys," their mom added, "you know that your dad and I work long hours and travel for our jobs, so we *need* someone to watch you."

Their dad picked it up from her as if they'd been rehearsing this speech. (They had.)

"But no matter whom we've hired, it always turns out the same. The caregivers always end up leaving our house and our lives too soon and just the way they found it—in chaos."

"According to the Nanny-o-Meter™ that I built for the science fair, we've *only* had seven hundred and thirty-four nannies," David insisted.

"That dumb thing never worked," Nathan told him. "I think it's actually three hundred and forty-seven."

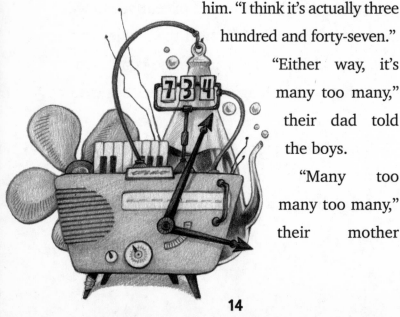

"Either way, it's many too many," their dad told the boys.

"Many too many too many," their mother

echoed, though technically that was a little confusing to everyone else in the room.

"I just can't understand why you guys seem to drive away every nanny we hire," their dad challenged them. "Can either of you give me a good reason why no one stays?"

"Dad, that's like asking why *L* is the twelfth letter of the alphabet," Nathan told him.

"Yeah, and it's like asking why all the World Series games are on TV too late to watch," David said.

Then Nathan and David took turns defending themselves.

Nathan: "Dad, not *all* of them left because of David and me. Don't you remember that Margo left because she won the lottery?"

David: "Betty left because she *didn't* win the lottery."

Nathan: "Nina left because she only wanted to clean the house at four in the morning. She said, 'It's better to vacuum when the dust is asleep.'"

David: "Vicki left because she had a dream that she should be an Olympic bobsledder, even though she hated bobsleds and snow and claimed she'd been born in twenty-three different countries."

All of what the boys said was true. But the sad fact was that many of the nannies had said good-bye because of Nathan.

Many left because of David.

And many, many, many, many (many!) left because of Nathan and David.

Of course, each time a nanny departed, the house became just a bit emptier. Because in truth, each one had brought something special to the Wohlfardt household.

Crystal made great meatballs.

Marina threw perfect curveballs.

Ibi served juicy, round melon balls.

Donna threw perfect bowling balls.

Lulu packed the hardest snowballs. And Maria (the fourteenth Maria—they'd known quite a few) could pronounce any word backward without even thinking about it—a skill you'd have to agree is GNIZAMA.

And then there was the nanny they called Ms. Lauderdale; she left the family to move to Fort Jackson. Or maybe it was Ms. Jackson who left to move to Fort Lauderdale?

At any rate, Josephine had gone, and once again, again, *again,* the Wohlfardt family was without a nanny.

CHAPTER
FOUR

"Perhaps you could do less traveling," Mrs. Wohlfardt gently suggested to her husband one nanny-less evening.

"That would be hard, dear," he replied. "After all, I *am* an airline pilot. And the last time I checked, the airline insisted that I do my work while on the plane."

"I see," said Mrs. Wohlfardt.

"Maybe *you* could work fewer hours," Mr. Wohlfardt said to his wife.

"I'd love to, Bob," she answered. "But things are always so busy at Jordan, Jordan, Jordan, Jordan, and Glerk. And my hard work has really paid off; this year I've gotten two promotions, three raises, and a new desk chair."

"I'm very proud of you," Mr. Wohlfardt said.

"Thank you," Mrs. Wohlfardt replied. She appreciated the compliment (and really enjoyed the desk chair), but she was not happy at that moment.

In fact, poor Mrs. Wohlfardt was at her wit's end. Every reliable nanny agency in town was fresh out of nannies. She'd even called the Unreliable Nanny Agency, but the nanny they'd offered her had recently changed her name from Margaret Watson to "Hey, You—Get Away from Me, I've Got a Highly Contagious Rash!" And that didn't sound promising.

"Who will take care of my children and my home?" Mrs. Wohlfardt moaned as she ironed

David's grilled cheese sandwich. (She was the first to admit that housework wasn't her best talent.) Mrs. Wohlfardt continued to think. She thought and she thought. And while she thought, she also ironed Nathan's backpack filled with books, Mr. Wohlfardt's spare guitar strings, and the remote control from their new HDTV.

"What to do? What to do?" Mrs. Wohlfardt softly sang to herself. She needed someone new to help care for Nathan and David, even though she knew she would probably soon be in search of someone else. Someone more patient. Someone smarter. Someone nicer. Or less bobsleddy.

Mrs. Wohlfardt was so troubled that she called everyone in her phone book.

She called friends.

She called friends of friends.

She called relatives of friends of friends.

She called friends of relatives of friends, friends of relatives, and relatives of friends of relatives.

And as she planned to start calling relatives of relatives of some *strangers and enemies*, the boys began to think back to all the nannies who'd come before.

"Remember Maria, and Vanessa, and Anita, and Lara, and the second Maria, and the third Maria, and the second Vanessa, and the first Maria when she came back after the second Vanessa?" Nathan said as he stared at the ceiling, because he'd once seen a movie in which people looked up when they were remembering the past.

"And Susan?" David added.

Nathan looked at his brother quizzically. "Wait, we had a Susan?"

"Remember between Anita and Lara, there was that red-haired lady who chewed tons of gum?"

"That was Susan? I thought she said her name was Blerblemowcha," said Nathan.

"It was Susan," said David. "It only sounded like Blerblemowcha because of the giant wad of gum in her mouth. She stayed here, like, two days. Then she spit out the gum, cleared her throat, and said she was leaving."

"Yup," said Nathan. "She just spit and quit."

As the boys rolled on the floor laughing at the joke, the

phone rang. Mrs. Wohlfardt answered it and immediately breathed a giant sigh of relief. When she hung up, she spoke the eight words that said, *Oh no, here we go again* in the minds of her twin boys.

"The new nanny will be here in the morning!"

CHAPTER
FIVE

It was a dark and stormy start to what would be a dark and stormy Saturday. Thunder rattled the dishes on the breakfast table.

"Are you sure the Martin Healey Discount Childcare Agency is sending someone trustworthy?" Mr. Wohlfardt asked his wife.

"Of course, dear," she answered. "After all, their slogan is 'When it comes to your kids, we don't kid around.' And the man on the phone sounded so sincere."

David gulped nervously. "I have a brilliant idea! You could just pay me to watch Nathan," he said.

"No! You could pay me to watch David," Nathan said. "Of course, I'd have to charge a lot *more*, because he's a brat. . . ."

"I am not!"

"You am too!"

"Hey!"

"Hey!"

"Stop that this instant," Mrs. Wohlfardt insisted. "You boys *must* stop fighting all the time!"

"But we can't stop fighting unless we start fighting first, right, Mom?" Nathan asked her.

The thought made sense to David, but it also kind of gave him a headache.

"Men, guys, boys," their dad continued. "You simply have to put an end to your truly unruly behavior."

"Truly unruly," Mrs. Wohlfardt repeated. "That's so poetic, my dear, and quite an excellent description."

Mr. Wohlfardt smiled at his wife; he was grateful that she noticed what a terrific rhymer he was. He made a mental note to start including rhymes in his announcements to passengers when he was piloting. He was thinking about rhyming pairs such as "flight-night" and "airline-hairline" when David brought him back to the conversation at hand.

"Tell me one thing we do wrong," David said.

"You fight. You're messy. You don't do your schoolwork on time and you leave things until the last minute," Mrs. Wohlfardt said.

"I asked you to tell me *one* thing," David said.

"Listen, you're not babies anymore," their dad offered. "You need to treat each other better, and you need to pay more attention to your responsibilities, at school and also at home. The way you both act, I don't blame our past nannies for wanting to work anywhere but here."

"And listen, boys," Mrs. Wohlfardt continued. "If either of you gives our new nanny reason to leave, this year's annual family ski trip will be canceled. Do you hear me? Canceled!"

"You can't cancel the annual family ski trip!" David insisted (a little louder than he'd meant to).

"Yeah, the annual family ski trip is the biggest thing we have to look forward to!" Nathan added.

David said, "We went last year. We went the year before that. And the year before that. And the year before that. . . ."

Afraid that David was going to put everyone to sleep by repeating that same sentence, Nathan jumped in.

"It's called an annual trip because it happens *annually*. Like, every year."

"Keep up your bad behavior and it'll be called the annual *canceled* ski trip," their dad told them. "And that's not just a threat, it's a promise."

"I hope you're hearing us. This year's trip will not happen if our new nanny runs out of the house screaming 'I can't stand these boys!'" their mom said.

"Right," Dad said. "And it will not happen if the nanny runs out screaming '*Jag kan inte står dessa pojkar!*'"

"Wonderful Swedish pronunciation, dear," said Mrs. Wohlfardt. "No one can say 'I cannot stand these boys' in Swedish better than you."

"Thank you, sweetie," Mr. Wohlfardt said with a smile. "But remember, I learned it from several of our nannies."

"*Min bror är en gris*," said Nathan. "That's Swedish too."

"How wonderful that you're speaking a foreign language!" Mrs. Wohlfardt beamed. "Tell me, Nathan . . . what does that mean?"

"It's Swedish for 'My brother is a pig.'" Nathan giggled.

"GO TO YOUR ROOM! BOTH OF YOU!" insisted Mrs. Wohlfardt.

"Hey! What did *I* do?" asked David.

"Go!" insisted Mr. Wohlfardt (with a slightly Swedish accent).

The boys stomped upstairs, elbowing each other to be first to get to a place they didn't really want to go to.

And just as Nathan and David reached their room, the lights suddenly flickered and went out.

Outside, hurricane winds screeched and screamed. Thunder crashed and lightning forked. A torrential rain poured.

As the dining room chandeliers began to clash and shake, the doorbell rang. One long, loud

BZZZ_{zzzz}z_{zz}ZZ_{zz}ZZZ_{zzz}!!!

"Go away! Nobody's home!" Nathan yelled as he and his brother pushed and tripped their way through the mass of wrinkled clothes, broken toys, crumpled papers, and dirty dishes on their floor and scrambled under their beds.

"Yes, go now and save yourself the trouble of having to leave us later!" David called.

But no nanny had ever braved such a fierce storm to get to the Wohlfardt house. No nanny had ever buzzed that long or that hard. What was happening? The boys had no idea. But they knew one thing—this new nanny was not going to be like any other!

CHAPTER
SIX

A booming voice echoed all the way up the stairs, down the hallway, into the twins' room, and under their beds. "Good day, I'm here from the Martin Healey Discount Childcare Agency."

"She sounds short and warty," whispered Nathan.

"Also hairy and weird," whispered David.

"And mean, grumpy, crabby, grouchy, irritable, and cranky!" added Nathan, having just found his long-lost thesaurus under the bed, not to mention an old but still tasty salami sandwich (which could possibly, just possibly, have been peanut butter).

"Let's stay under here forever," continued Nathan. "That way we'll never have to meet her, and she can just slip our meals under the door."

"Amazing idea! We can live on pancakes and bologna slices," David offered.

"And pizza," Nathan added. "She could definitely slide thin-crust pizza."

David was about to argue that the cheese would stick to the bottom of the door, when his mom interrupted.

"Boys, come down and meet someone new!" she cheerily chirped from downstairs.

"New nanny! Move your fanny! Er, fann*ies*," added Dad, who clearly needed to work on that rhyme.

Sensing there was no way out, the boys moped down the stairs to meet the next lady who would be running, er, *ruining* their lives.

Nathan reached the bottom of the stairs first.

He stopped and gasped.

David, who was right behind him, was so surprised that he fell off the last step. They tumbled onto the floor in a heap.

The boys were speechless. This person was neither short nor warty. As for weird—well, that was extremely possible. Because the first thing they noticed was . . .

. . . a big, bushy mustache! In fact, it was a mushy, bushy mustache, which is a good tongue-twister but a horrible look. And while one or two of their previous nannies had mustaches, this was quite different. Because more than anything, what struck Nathan and David right away was . . . this nanny was clearly, 100 percent, undeniably, without a doubt . . .

CHAPTER
SEVEN

. . . A MANNY!

"Greetings! Have a nice trip? See you next fall!" the new person said in a crisp British accent as he helped them to their feet.

He scratched his bushy mustache and pointed to Nathan. "You must be Miranda," he said. "Which of course makes *you* Petunia!" he said to David.

"I'm Nathan," said Nathan. "And this is my brother, um, Petunia."

"I am not Petunia!" said David. "I'm David."

"Yes, of course. And I'm your new best friend from the Martin Healey Discount Child-care Agency," the man said, exactly as he had before. Then he smoothed his mustache. "Martin Healey is the name."

"Do you own the agency?" their father asked.

"I *am* the agency," said Martin.

"Why is it the Martin Healey *Discount* Childcare Agency?" their mother wanted to know. "Are you on sale, marked down like the dented can of peaches I get for twenty-five cents off at the market, Martin?"

"Are you past your freshness date? We must have only the freshest nanny," their father insisted.

"I assure you, I am one-hundred-percent fresh grade-A merchandise. And to answer your question, my name is Martin Healey

Discount—a direct descendant of the Royal Discount Monarchy of Ex-Laxingberg."

"Don't you mean Ex-Luxembourg?" Mr. Wohlfardt wanted to know. "Or, er, ah, ahem—I mean . . . Luxembourg?"

"Precisely, my good fellow," said Martin. "I'd forgotten the Americanized pronunciation. Do pardon."

"Royalty? My goodness!" Mrs. Wohlfardt beamed. "Did you hear that, boys? With this nanny, you're in the presence of world leadership!"

"Madam, while you may consider Martin Healey Discount a mere nanny, I am, in fact, so much more. I am what you call . . ." He cleared his throat. "A T-A-B-A-S-C-O," Martin spelled, his mustache wriggling on every letter.

"Tabasco?" asked David. "Like the sauce?"

"No, my dear boy," Martin continued. "It's an acronym. Letters that represent words.

I'm a highly trained Teacher and Babysitter and Scholarly Childcare Orchestrator. It's an extremely important title earned through more years of schooling than one could possibly complete in a lifetime."

"Speaking of letters, do you have letters of recommendation?" Mr. Wohlfardt asked Martin.

"Why, yes, I do, I most certainly do," Martin told him. "Would you like to see the letter written about me by the emperor of—*cough, cough, cough*—or the ambassador of—*ahem, ahem, ahem*—or the duchess of—*hiccup, hiccup, hiccup*?"

"You worked for all those people?" Nathan wanted to know.

"Lived with? Yes. Cared for? Most certainly. Became a family member of? Indeed. But *worked*? Only in the sense that they employed me and paid me to be there, young gent."

Mr. and Mrs. Wohlfardt were quite impressed by the thought that Martin had been considered a family member by all his previous employers—even though that's not exactly what he'd said.

"Hey, your hiccups stopped!" David said. "So did your coughing and throat clearing."

"The respect and admiration I feel inside this glorious home have cured me of all ills, I suspect," he told Nathan and David. "Yes, this feels like a warm, wonderful, well-built home."

Mrs. Wohlfardt was grinning from ear to ear.

The boys, however, were not.

"Are you fun?" asked Nathan.

"Fun, my dear boy? Fun?" Martin frowned as he poked Nathan in the nose to punctuate every word. "That's perfectly preposterous! Totally tiresome! And tremendously pellinomous!"

Nathan was quite sure "pellinomous" wasn't a word. (It's not.) But more important, the boy was soaking wet, because besides poking, Martin spit a little with each word containing the letters *P* and *T*.

"You ask about fun, Sir Nathan?" Martin continued. "Why, *fun* is a by-product of irresponsibility. It's perfectly clear that school chores, home chores, family chores, and life-improvement chores are your primary responsibility. Strict attention must be paid to schedule, to completing tasks such as homework, to studying, room tidying, proper hygiene, nutrition, and being a solid citizen and loving friend to your brother, your parents, and those around you in perpetuity!"

The boys gulped and wiped away the *P* and *T* spit.

"Then," Martin continued again, "if there's any time left over, we may attempt to explore this concept of fun. Do we understand each other, men?"

Nathan and David looked like they'd both swallowed raw squid wrapped in raw onions coated in hot chili peppers. But Mr. and Mrs. Wohlfardt were absolutely thrilled at everything Martin Healey Discount had said.

As a finishing touch, Martin dug into his suitcase and pulled out one dozen long-stemmed roses for Mrs. Wohlfardt.

"Roses! My favorite! How did you know, Martin?" Mrs. Wohlfardt asked him.

"Good guess," said Martin. "It is my fondest wish that you enjoy them, Mrs. Wohl*fardt*," he added, for some reason speaking softly on the "Wohl" and loudly on the "fardt."

Then Martin reached into his suitcase again and pulled out a football signed by all the Denver Broncos for Mr. Wohlfardt.

"The Denver Broncos?" Mr. Wohlfardt exclaimed. "My number one team!"

"Indeed," said Martin.

"What about *us*?" Nathan and David asked.

Martin reached into the suitcase one last time. "For you young gentlemen," Martin exclaimed, "I have two finely crafted, precision . . . toothbrushes! Now run along upstairs and brush your teeth!"

"But it's ten thirty in the morning!" Nathan complained. "We never brush at ten thirty in the morning!"

"Cavities cannot tell time, Squire. We must defeat them by exercising proper dental care around the clock! Now go!" Martin insisted. "And upon completion of this important hygiene task, please organize your dresser drawers and then your schoolwork for a thorough inspection!"

This was too much to bear.

"A *zombie commando babysitter* is moving into our house!" David said. "We're sunk!"

"Is this a joke? Are we being secretly filmed for a prank reality show?" Nathan nervously tossed a pink bouncy ball against the wall.

"A joke? Hardly, young man! I am quite serious. I have no interest in being on—or watching—that time-wasting, life-sucking device known as the telly. Or 'television,' as you call it."

Mr. and Mrs. Wohlfardt grinned. They could not believe their good fortune in finding Martin. He was truly the caretaker of their dreams!

"Furthermore, as for bouncing that round, orblike object you hold in your hand—we simply do not do that in the interior of the premises," he said, spitting out all his *P*s and *T*s and taking the ball from Nathan.

"It will be returned to you during a future outdoor recreation session."

The elder Wohlfardts tried not to grin as Nathan sadly watched his ball disappear into Martin's side pocket.

"Now upstairs, you two! Brush those teeth! *Tish-spot!*" Martin barked, which somehow made his mustache whirl and twirl like a motion-sickness-causing carnival ride.

For the second time that morning, the boys found themselves being sent upstairs. And when they reached the landing, they found they finally agreed on something—an overwhelming sense of doom, now that the new nanny had arrived at their house.

"This is *the worst!*" said Nathan. "I can't believe mom and dad hired *The Mustache!*"

"Yeah," David moaned. "Out of all the millions of nannies in this world, why, oh why, did *Murray Poopins* have to land in *our* living room?"

CHAPTER EIGHT

Moments later, the boys had brushed their teeth and begun organizing their dresser drawers and their schoolwork as they had been told. They could hear Martin pushing large objects around in the Wohlfardt guest room. As they listened to about six truckloads of furniture being moved into that fairly tiny room, the boys thought it sure seemed as if he was planning a long stay.

Nathan and David were in a total panic as they reviewed their very limited options. There was no time for their usual petty arguing; they had to unite to confront the enemy.

"We need to get rid of this guy ... fast!" David said as he picked up a lampshade from the floor, tossed it in the air, and tried to catch it on his head.

"Yeah," said Nathan, using a flyswatter as a bubble wand and intentionally filling his brother's hair with soap bubbles. "Fast!"

"But if we get rid of him, there's no ski trip," said David, tossing the lampshade again.

"And no hot tub or eighty-five-inch TV in our room," added Nathan.

"Mom and Dad never said anything about those things," David told him.

"They did to me. Only to me," Nathan insisted. "I think those things will be in here after they send you to live in the rain forest."

"Stop that! Pay attention!" David scolded his brother.

"I hate to admit it, but you're right," Nathan said, stroking his chin as he'd seen deep thinkers do on TV. "We've got to hatch a genius plot that makes it seem as if Martin *has to leave* . . . but it can't look like it's because of us, because that could give Mom and Dad a reason to take away the ski trip!"

"I hate to admit it, but good point," David said, squeezing his face to think harder than he'd done since, well, ever. "Think, think, think, think, think . . ."

"I can't think if you keep saying 'think,'" Nathan told him. "Less talking, more thinking, will ya?"

"Um, we could send him an urgent e-mail saying that 'Sir Luxingburp' is needed to run his family's country," David suggested as he folded his underwear, until he realized it was Nathan's and flung it onto his brother's head.

"Or . . . we could leave a message at the Martin Healey Discount Childcare Agency offering him a million dollars a week to come work somewhere else," Nathan said as he removed clumped-up modeling clay and several mashed-up test papers from the extremely deep bottom of his extremely sticky backpack.

"Great idea," said David. "But where could we possibly get a million dollars a week?"

"I don't know," said Nathan. "I have about sixty dollars from our birthday money, and you have forty dollars. . . ."

"We each got fifty dollars," David said.

"Yes, but I took ten dollars from your piggy bank when you weren't looking," Nathan admitted.

David was too upset about the new nanny to complain about the theft.

"Well," David said, "together we have one hundred dollars. And that's, like, almost ten thousand short of a million."

"Excellent job on your math, Mr. Genius," Nathan responded. "Actually, a million minus one hundred leaves nine hundred thousand, nine hundred dollars."

"Actually, *your* math is very boring. The point is we don't have enough," David told him.

"No, the point is on the top of your head," Nathan answered.

David ignored Nathan's comment.

"Ugh. My teeth feel weird," David said.

He ran his tongue over them.

"Like, *too* clean."

"Yeah, mine too," replied his brother.

"Our lives are over," David moaned.

"Over!" Nathan agreed as they plopped down on their beds to rest.

"Man-oh-manny, does this guy have to go," said David. "Man-oh-manny-man-man . . ."

No one knows how long David was going to keep saying that nonsense phrase. Because he stopped when the bedroom door suddenly blew open. Amid a swirl of sparkly dust, there stood. . .

CHAPTER
NINE

. . . Martin Healey Discount!

"Seems I have caught you gentlemen in a moment of relaxation," Martin observed. "Am I to assume you've completed your assigned tasks?"

"I-I—um, er . . . ," said David.

"We, um, ah, well . . . ," added Nathan.

"Remember," Martin boomed, "as my great-grandfather the Royal Adam of Sandler once told me, 'A boy who shirks work does not earn a perk!' No fun for you! *Tish-posh!*"

"I-I—um, er . . . ," said David.

"We, um, ah, well . . . ," Nathan added as Martin stepped all the way into their room and closed the door.

The boys froze, until Martin whispered in a clearly non-British accent:

"Relax, you crazy loons! I was just kiddin' ya! Work? Ha! Chores? Blah! Hygiene? Responsibility? Fuggetaboudit!"

"Huh?" said the boys.

"It's all a big act to impress your parents!" Martin said.

Then he pulled Nathan's ball out of his pocket, spun it on his fingertip, bounced it off the wall,

ceiling,

floor,

ceiling,

floor,

wall,

and right into Nathan's hands.

Then Martin giggled.

"You're not from royalty?" David asked.

"I'm from Brooklyn, New York," Martin answered.

"You're not a nutrition nut?" asked Nathan.

"I had seven Toaster Tarts and three bowls of Loopy Fruits for breakfast!"

"What about all that talk about school-work? Are you gonna make us study nonstop?" David asked.

"Do we have to do chores all the time?"

David wanted to know. "Or keep brushing our teeth?"

"Relax, guys. As for studying, tidying, and brushinginging, that's not who I am. Listen, I haven't yet memorized all twenty-four letters of the alphabet! I haven't flossed since 1992! Never did give a hoot about my breath, which on a good day smells like my armpits!" Martin laughed and slapped his thighs. "I can't believe you guys fell for all that! What a pair of suckers!"

He breathed on the plant in the corner and it immediately withered and collapsed.

"Wait, so why'd you make us brush our teeth?" David asked.

"And clean our dresser drawers?" Nathan continued.

Martin giggled. "Oh, that." He giggled again. "Don't you see what fun we can have? In front of your parents, I'll be the caregiver of the century, the king of responsibility. But when we're alone, it's going to be good times all the time!" He giggled again.

This seemed too good to be true.

"But you've got to play along with it," Martin continued. "When your parents are around and I tell you to brush your teeth, you have to do it. If I say, 'Scrub the floors,' then you have to do that, too. Understood?"

The boys nodded.

Then Martin handed them each a piece of paper. "Here's the daily schedule. . . ."

The boys read to themselves, competing, as usual, to see who could finish first.

1. Parents go to work
2. TV, TV, TV
3. Indoor tennis in the living room
4. Massive unhealthy snack
5. TV, TV, TV
6. Jumping on the beds

7. Hide-and-seek

8. TV, TV, TV

9. Bubblegum-blowing competition on the white couch

10. TV

11. Stand-on-your-head juggling class with good crystal

12. Deep-fried triple-chocolate snack

13. More TV

"What about school?" David wanted to know.

"I don't go to school," Martin answered.

"But *we* do," David insisted. "We have to."

"It's the law!" said Nathan.

"Hmm. I suppose you'll have to go, then," Martin answered. "Okay, that's just a small disruption; we'll fit it in somehow. So this will just be *my* daily schedule . . . though I *hate* playing indoor tennis all by myself." He giggled. "Now listen, you nut jobs! We're going to have so much fun!"

Martin gave them a crazy salute, opened the door, and backed out of the room. But right before he closed the door, he pointed to a pile of books on the boys' desks and said (loud enough for Mr. and Mrs. Wohlfardt to hear, of course), "Remember, there's a 'u' in the center of the word 'study.' And that 'u' stands for *you*! Study on!"

The door slammed shut and Martin was gone.

Nathan looked at David. David looked at Nathan. They opened their books and began to study.

Could it be true? A babysitter who lived for TV, junk food, and jumping on the beds? At that moment, it seemed extremely possible that Martin Healey Discount could be the world's best nanny! But for now, they had to spend the rest of the night doing homework.

CHAPTER
TEN

The next morning, Martin woke Nathan and David at 5:15 a.m. Exhausted from a night of study and homework, they could barely move.

"Arise, young gents," Martin announced as he rapidly rap-tap-tapped on their bedroom door. "Remember, it is the early bird that catches the worm."

"Who needs a worm?" David mumbled and grumbled to himself. But there was no use arguing; he knew that seeming to be responsible was all part of the deal they'd made with Martin.

At precisely five thirty, the freshly showered duo of Nathan and David Wohlfardt dragged themselves down the stairs and slid into their seats at the empty breakfast table.

The boys stared in disbelief. Where was the junk food Martin had promised them?

Martin delicately slid three eggs out from his shirt pocket. "Behold three glorious eggs. Two are deliciously, nutritiously hard-boiled, and the other one's raw," he said while juggling them at blinding speed. "Choose wisely and you'll have breakfast. Make the wrong choice, and the yolk's on you!" He giggled.

"You pick first!" Nathan said.

"No, you!" answered David.

"You!"

"You!"

This went on for a while, until Martin solved the problem by having the boys go in alphabetical order—by the last letters of their middle names (Nathan Reuben went before David Meyer).

Nathan chose and got a hard-boiled egg.

David chose and also got a hard-boiled egg.

Then Martin cracked the third egg, which in fact was also hard-boiled, and he peeled and ate it.

Martin had tricked them into eating a healthy breakfast!

After breakfast, they still had more than two hours until they had to be in school. Martin told them delightful stories about his own delightful childhood, sharing tales of how his nanny made sure he got to school delightfully early so he could get a delightful seat in the delightful classroom. The boys found none of this delightful, except perhaps that the nanny's name was Harriet D. Lightful.

After that, Martin led the boys through an exercise routine (he watched, they exercised), had them study some more (he watched, they studied), and then joined them to tidy up their room (he watched, they tidied).

Nathan and David were pretty upset over how the morning was going. They thought their "deal" with Martin meant free time and playtime all the time, but here they were doing all things that were decidedly undelightful.

"Martin must be making us do all this so Mom and Dad will be impressed," Nathan whispered to David as he dusted his collection of "Your Team Lost But You Get a Giant Trophy Anyway" giant trophies.

"Yeah, I guess you're right," David said. "But *impressing* them is *depressing* me!"

"Enough dilly-dolly-dallying," Martin called out so everyone in town could hear. Then he hustled both boys off to school sixty minutes before the first bell.

When he returned, Mr. and Mrs. Wohlfardt met him at the front door.

"You are remarkable with the boys, Martin," Mrs. Wohlfardt told him.

"Remarkable *and* quite hark-able," added Mr. Wohlfardt, willing to sacrifice logical meaning for a cute-ish rhyme. "I never thought I'd see our twins so motivated to exercise, study, clean up, and get to school on time!"

"You're a real treasure, Martin," Mrs. Wohlfardt said. "We thank you for being here, Martin," she added, and suddenly realized that everything she had ever said to him ended with the word "Martin." She vowed to stop that.

"I would still, of course, like to read those letters of recommendation," Mr. Wohlfardt said.

"Letters, yes, letters," Martin said, hurriedly helping Mr. and Mrs. Wohlfardt with their coats, briefcases, lunches, and assorted other items designed to get them out of the house as soon as possible. "I would be glad to prepare and produce those letters of recommendation at once. However, as a wise man once said, 'To be late for work is to be late for life.' You both must go now. At once! *Tish-poof!* Mind those planes, sir. Mind your business, ma'am."

As he spoke, Martin practically pushed them out the door. But rather than feeling rushed, rather than being upset over not seeing the recommendation letters, Mr. and Mrs. Wohlfardt actually appreciated Martin's concern.

"Arriva-dusty!" Martin called after the pair as he watched them drive away.

Once Mr. and Mrs. Wohlfardt were gone, the house was quiet. And Martin was . . . tired. Thinking about his job and his responsibilities, he did the only thing he could think to do at that moment: he went back to his room and slept until noon.

CHAPTER
ELEVEN

NANNY—AN INTERNATIONAL SPY!
read the front-page headline on the local newspaper a few weeks after Martin's arrival.

Martin had dropped the boys off at the
library that afternoon, after telling Mr. and Mrs.
Wohlfardt, "The boys have a playdate this afternoon with William Shakespeare, Mark Twain,
and that lovely young man Charles Dickens."

"Look at this!" David said to Nathan,
shoving the newspaper in his face.

"What? Wow! 'Missing doggy found,'" Nathan read aloud. "Thrilling."

"Not that!" David said. "Higher up."

"'Mayor approves trash collection budget'?" Nathan asked. "Big deal!"

"Still higher up!" David insisted.

"'Nanny—an international spy.' Yeah, so what?"

"That could be Martin," David said. "What if Martin is an international spy?"

"He's not," answered Nathan, studying the paper. "It says the spy's name is Max Heller Douglas."

"How many nannies do you think are mannies? And this is a case of mannies with the same initials!" David said. "Max Heller Douglas is MHD, and so is Martin Healey Discount!"

"Just coincidence," Nathan told his brother. "It also says that Max Heller Douglas was a nanny for girls named Natalie Wilson and Dana Wilson."

"Spooky! Those are the same initials again!" David said with mystery in his voice. "NW like Nathan Wohlfardt, and DW like David Wohlfardt!"

"Two more coincidences, I'm sure," Nathan told him. "And look, it says that Max Heller Douglas is seven feet tall and doesn't have a mustache. So there. Martin is more than a foot shorter, and he *does* have a mustache."

"Ah, but how do we know it's a real mustache?" David wondered. "Maybe he takes it off at night. And maybe he's here to spy on our family."

"I never thought I'd say this to you, David," Nathan said, "but I think you're thinking too much. Go back to the way you usually are."

"If he *is* a spy, we've got to tell Mom and Dad," David warned.

"If he is, which he's not, and we tell, which we won't, and he leaves, which he shouldn't, then we don't get the ski trip, which we should," Nathan said.

"Yes, but if he is, which he could be, and we don't tell, which we should, and he stays, which he shouldn't, and he gives away all our family secrets, which he might, then what?" David wanted to know.

"Our only family secret is that you're a nut," Nathan told him. "And honestly, it's not that much of a secret."

"Nathan, your problem is that you trust people too much. Remember how you didn't believe me when I said Ibi was from another planet . . . until we found her Interplanetary Citizenship Card?"

"She got that when she joined the *Star Blazers* TV show fan club," Nathan told him.

"Logical excuse. But deep down, I still suspect she was a super-creepy space alien from the planet Zelba!" David insisted.

"Stop being so suspicious, David. The only one around here from another planet is you!" Nathan said.

"Laugh if you want to, Nathan. But I know a spy when I meet one, and . . ."

David looked toward the ceiling and thrust his right arm into the air for emphasis as he spoke louder than you really should in a library.

"Martin Healey Discount, Super-Spy . . . I'm onto you!"

CHAPTER
TWELVE

One afternoon later that week, Nathan came home from school with the exciting news that he'd been picked as a candidate for class president. His mother didn't know yet. His father didn't know yet. Even his brother probably didn't know yet, because he was busy attending an after-school model-building class, putting the finishing touches on something that was either a two-foot-long replica of the *Titanic* or an extremely ugly giant wooden gecko.

"You know, I was class president three times," Martin told Nathan. "Twice in fourth grade, and once in fifth grade."

"You were in fourth grade twice?" Nathan asked.

"Actually, *three* times," Martin answered. "In my school, we went to first, then fourth, then second, then fourth, then third, then fourth, then seventh."

"Is that true?" Nathan asked.

"I'm sorry, I wasn't listening to a single thing I was saying," Martin told him. "But, Nathan, if you expect to win the school election, you are going to need good campaign signs."

"Well, I—" Nathan started.

Martin interrupted him. "And speaking of good signs, it's a good sign that I'm available to be your official campaign manager," Martin said. "Here's your first slogan: 'Give Your Whole Heart to Nathan Wohlfardt!'"

"Aw, that sounds like a Valentine's Day card, Martin," Nathan said. "I want votes, not hugs."

"Listen, friend," Martin told him. "Anyone with the last name of Wohlfardt should consider himself lucky to have a slogan at all."

Nathan made a sour face.

"Next, we'll work on your buttons and your bumper stickers," Martin said.

"Bumper stickers?" Nathan asked. "But kids in my school don't drive cars!"

"Exactly!" Martin brightened. "That's why it's such a good idea—none of the other candidates will think of that!"

"Think of *what*?" David asked as he entered the room with his usual slam-dunk-the-doorframe leap.

"Bumper stickers," Nathan answered.

"Don't be ridiculous, *you* didn't think of bumper stickers!" David said. "Forest P. Gill

invented them back in the 1930s!" he added, having recently read that in a book of little-known facts.

"No, you dinker-head! We're talking about making bumper stickers for the election campaign!" Nathan told him. "To go along with the posters!"

"You're already making posters for the election?" David asked. *"But how did you know I'm running?"*

"Men, this is not the first time in history that siblings have run for the same office,"

Martin said as he stood between the presidential rivals. "George Washington beat his brother Irving, Abraham Lincoln was elected over his brother Milton, and Millard Fillmore defeated his brothers Willard, Dillard, and Schmillard."

David and Nathan were pretty sure that Martin was being far more hysterical than historical. But before they could challenge him, Mrs. Wohlfardt entered the room.

"Good afternoon, madame," Martin said, suddenly standing at attention and licking cookie crumbs off his mustache. "We were just reviewing our historical facts."

"Homework, Martin?" she asked.

"On the contrary," Martin answered. "Pleasure learning! As I've repeatedly told the gents, history should not be a mystery, for tomorrow is merely the future of the past tense of what hasn't yet happened."

Mrs. Wohlfardt looked puzzled but was impressed at the same time.

"The splendid news," Martin continued, "is that you are raising not one but two potential class presidents!"

"My goodness!" Mrs. Wohlfardt grinned. "I'm so proud of my boys!" She beamed and kissed them both good-bye.

Martin took a deep breath, grabbed a poster marker, and charted the situation:

"Okay, let's figure this out. Two brothers. Two candidates. One wins, one loses. How exciting that someone from this white-and-brown house will soon occupy the school's White House!"

"Um, the school doesn't actually *have* a White House," Nathan told him.

But that didn't really matter to Martin, who was as deep in thought as he could get without looking and smelling like an overheating car engine.

Martin thought and thought and thought for nearly six seconds before exclaiming . . .

"I've got it! Men, think about it. What's the one thing an ordinary person needs to attain the top office?"

"Honesty?" Nathan guessed.

"Responsibility?" David offered.

"Courage?" Nathan tried.

"Compassion?" David said.

"Not even close!" Martin insisted. "To go from resident to president, all a person needs is the letter *P*. Get it? P-resident. P-resident. President!"

"How does that help us?" Nathan wanted to know (while ducking Martin's repeated *P*-spit sprays).

"It doesn't. Not a bit," Martin admitted. "But now that I've demonstrated how masterful I am with words, it's time for you to ask me to write your campaign speeches for you."

"Thanks, but I don't need to have a written campaign speech. I'll figure out what I'm going to say when I get there tomorrow," Nathan said.

"Me too," said David. "And what I come up with will be better and clearer than whatever blabbering we'll hear from my unworthy, smelly opponent, who just happens to be my unworthy, smelly twin brother."

"Oh yeah?" Nathan yelled.

"Yeah!" David yelled back.

"We'll see about that!"

"Yes, we will!"

"Oh yeah?"

"Yeah!"

"We'll see about that!"

"Yes, we will!"

The boys continued arguing in a repetitive, uncreative way for a really, really long time. They eventually got too tired to fight, and each

twin spent the evening working on his campaign speech. Well, actually, they were both
just endlessly doodling the words "Campaign
Speech" on a pad.

Martin stayed away from the boys all night;
he was in his room, snacking on a large tray of
tomato and tomato sandwiches (don't ask) and
bellowing, "Martin, you are a genius!" every
3.2 minutes.

CHAPTER
THIRTEEN

Every seat in the school auditorium was filled. There was even someone sitting in row seven, seat three, which no one had occupied since the Great Prune Danish Incident back in 2012.

The size of the crowd clearly showed how important this election was to the school.

Two candidates.

Two podiums.

And one Mrs. Peyser, who stepped to the microphone and announced, "Good morning, everyone. In a few minutes, you'll be hearing from David Wohlfardt and Nathan Wohlfardt, our two presidential candidates. But first, please rise and let's sing the school song."

The students (except Nathan, who, if you remember, hates singing) stood up and sang:

Let's all hail Screamersville Slightly Northeast
    Elementary School
It's a good place to learn
A whole lifetime long
Yes, let's all hail Screamersville Slightly Northeast
    Elementary School
And now, let's stop singing this song!

All the students knew that the song hardly made sense, but Mrs. Peyser had written it, and no one wanted to hurt her feelings. So they sang it at every assembly.

"Okay, everyone," Mrs. Peyser announced. "Please welcome David and Nathan to the podiums."

The boys went to their assigned spots. David looked out at the sea of faces—pretty much everyone he'd ever met—and gulped hard. Instead of thinking of a ton of worthwhile things to say, he felt his mind go 100 percent blank.

At the other podium, Nathan was experiencing the same sensation of panic.

Nathan looked at David and smiled nervously.

David looked at Nathan and smiled nervously.

David was sure that when he opened his mouth, he'd only make creaks and squeaks.

Nathan was sure that he was about to drool out a whole bunch of gibberish. In fact, for some reason, the phrase "Me like mashy potatoes" kept repeating in his head, and he was pretty sure that was going to be his opening line. And his second line. And his whole speech.

Fortunately (well, sort of), right before either boy could speak, Mrs. Peyser said something rather incredible.

"Oh, boys," she said. "I almost forgot! Someone named Martin came by this morning and gave me these folders with your speeches in them! In your excitement, you both left them home this morning!"

With that, she handed each boy a folder. Stapled on the cover of Nathan's folder was a sheet of paper that said:

Hey, Nath,

I was afraid to let you speak without having anything prepared. So here's a real speech, much like the one I wrote for President Bill Clinton, though he never knew anything about it.

Love,
Martin

And on David's folder was a sheet of paper that said:

Hey, Davy Wavy Gravy,

You were too lazy to write anything down, and that made me worry about ya. So here's a real speech, much like the one I wrote for my own pal Jim Gooberman on the night he was elected prom queen.

Admiringlylylyly,
Martin

Mrs. Peyser smiled and said, "Okay, Nathan, based on the fact that I have a cousin whose next-door neighbor's middle name is Nathan, I have selected you to speak first."

Nathan knew that there was no turning back. He stared at the crowd, then opened the folder and read what Martin had prepared for him.

"Good evening, ladies and germs. If elected, I promise to change this school in many thrilling ways. First, I will start a free—yes, free—pencil-sharpening service. Also, there will be no more homework. Everyone will get double desserts after lunch. We'll have four-day weekends every week. Summer will be eight months long. The gym will be turned into a 3-D movie theater. And, best of all, there'll be live rock concerts during tests. Thank you."

As Nathan reviewed the last few minutes in his mind—wondering, *What did I just say?*—the entire crowd cheered for an incredibly long time, and Mrs. Peyser didn't know whether to laugh or cry.

"Settle down, students," she called. Once they were quieter, she gestured to David. "David, you are next," she said, with a look in her eye that some students, though not David, might have seen as a warning.

David took a deep breath and read what Martin had crafted for him.

"Hello, fellow students. It is an honor and a privilege to be considered for the position of president in this most excellent school. I am humbled and honored by the chance to speak to you about how we, as students, might work alongside the wonderful faculty here to make this school an even more special place to learn."

A few kids snickered. A few others booed. But Mrs. Peyser smiled a wide smile and heaved a deep sigh of relief.

David continued, "And it is with that goal in mind that I offer the following campaign promises: If elected, I vow to insist that all answers to multiple-choice tests be 'A,' and the answers to all true-false questions be 'true.' I will also convince the teachers that anyone who spells any word right at any time gets to skip two grades. And from now on, the school day on Wednesdays will only be seven minutes long, with a recess break after three minutes. Furthermore—"

But Mrs. Peyser stood up and stopped David before he could get to his further-more (which, by the way, was the promise that he'd put a video arcade in every school bathroom).

Mrs. Peyser addressed David and Nathan with fire in her eyes. "Boys, these campaign promises are ridiculous, nonsensical, and unacceptable. I am asking you to leave the stage. I am asking you to leave the election. And you're lucky I am not asking you to leave the school."

"But . . . ," said David.

"But . . . ," said Nathan.

"I do not want to hear your 'buts'!" said Mrs. Peyser.

That statement, of course, was met with the loudest laughter ever heard in the auditorium at Screamersville Slightly Northeast Elementary School.

CHAPTER FOURTEEN

"Martin tricked us!" David said to Nathan when they were alone in the lunchroom after the assembly.

"Yeah, he tricked us!" Nathan agreed.

"Those ridiculous campaign promises cost me the election!" David said.

"Yeah, they cost me the election too!" Nathan agreed.

David continued, "Man, if Martin the Super-Spy hadn't dropped off those folders, I'd, I'd, I'd . . ."

"Yeah, I'd, I'd, I'd too . . . ," Nathan agreed.

"Who am I kidding? I hadn't prepared anything, and I was crazy nervous up there. No matter what Martin wrote, at least it gave me something to say," David admitted.

"Yeah, me too," Nathan told him. "The only thing I could think of was 'Me like mashy potatoes.'"

David snickered and said, "I'm not sure I would have even come up with that. So we probably both would have frozen and lost anyway, huh?"

"I guess so," Nathan said. "But why did Martin give us such ridiculous campaign promises?"

"Well, the kids loved them," David said. "Mrs. Peyser, not so much. And it was our fault that we weren't prepared."

"So in a way, Martin did us a favor?" Nathan wondered.

"Maybe. Yeah. No. I don't know," David offered. "But next time, I think we'd better do our work before he has to do it for us."

"You know, David," Nathan said, "sometimes you're not as stupid as you really are."

"And, Nathan," David answered, "sometimes you make me glad I have an annoying twin brother."

There was a long silence (which was rare for those guys).

"We almost had a nice moment of maturity there, didn't we?" asked Nathan.

"Yeah, almost," David said as he started to walk away. "Think it's because we're getting older?"

"Maybe," Nathan said. "But mostly I think it's because Martin's making us pay closer attention to stuff. The other nannies always just let us act as crazy and irresponsible as we wanted to, and then they'd leave. But Martin is different."

"Totally different," David said. "Look, he's even got us agreeing with each other and doing things together to protect the ski trip."

"Weird," Nathan said.

"Yeah, weird," David said as he took his tray and Nathan's and began walking toward the trash.

David had never done anything like that for his brother. When he realized what he was doing, he almost went back to put the tray down. But he kept going, turned his head, and called to his brother.

"Hey, Nathan," David yelled.

"Yeah?" Nathan asked.

"Me like mashy potatoes too!" David said.

Later that afternoon, when the election was held for school president, Nathan and David Wohlfardt didn't get a single vote. Instead, the winner of the election was the one and only Bobby Likpa—not because everyone thought he'd make a great leader, but because they were all so impressed he'd been able to make it through the whole assembly while sitting in row seven, seat three.

CHAPTER FIFTEEN

Whenever the boys were in school, Martin was all alone and sad inside the Wohlfardt residence. Like a sheepdog anxiously looking for its master, Martin simply couldn't wait for the boys to come home. He filled his time with his personally trademarked Find a New Activity Every 36 Minutes™ rule, spending pretty much every day with a series of extremely creative household chores. In fact, they were so creative, Martin was thinking of writing a book of household chores called *The Martin Healey Discount Book of Extremely Creative Household Chores.*

At 11:03 a.m., Martin prepared a meat loaf shaped like his head for the family dinner.

At 11:39 a.m., he vacuumed the den, then emptied the contents of the vacuum onto the living room floor and re-vacuumed.

At 12:15 p.m., he tested his "It's better to wash the dishes and the laundry in the same machine" theory.

At 12:51 p.m., he picked the broken glass and china out of the washing machine.

And at 1:27 p.m., he unraveled Mr. Wohl-fardt's favorite wool scarf and then re-knitted it, this time as a sweater.

Exactly thirty-six minutes later, realizing Mr. Wohlfardt might not like short-sleeved sweaters, he knitted it back into a scarf and wrapped it as a surprise gift.

Exactly thirty-six minutes after that, realizing that Mr. Wohlfardt might not think receiving his own scarf was much of a gift, he unwrapped it and put it back in the closet. Then he made a fresh, lemony tuna salad and washed the windows with it—after which he called it a day.

Martin was bored. And lonely.

"You know, Marty old boy, old chap, old man, old boy, old socks," he told himself, "you need a hobby. Perhaps you could discover a new chemical element. Or paint a painting. Or paint the deck. Or deck the halls. Or haul out the trash. Or learn to ride a bucking bronco while carrying a soufflé."

After considering many options, Martin finally decided that he didn't need a real hobby after all; hearing his own voice made him happier than any activity possibly could. So he kept talking to himself about many strangely fascinating topics until the boys came home.

CHAPTER
SIXTEEN

At three fifteen, Martin was crouching on the floor by the front door, peering through the mail slot and waiting for Nathan and David to arrive. The tuna had made the windows a bit foggy. And not surprisingly, it had also made them smell like tuna fish. By the time the boys finally got home, Martin had excitedly eaten up all the milk and cookies he'd put out for them.

"Hey, guys! Welcome home!" Martin greeted them. "Which one of you is president?"

"Neither of us," David told him.

"Yeah, neither of us," Nathan echoed. "Martin, about those speeches . . ."

"Don't thank me, gents! My pleasure!" Martin said. "And sorry about the election, boys. But I'm proud to announce something more important than winning a school election and basking in the admiration of your whole student body!"

The boys couldn't wait to hear what Martin was going to say next.

"Boys, put the vote out of your cute little minds, because . . . it's playtime! Playtime! Time to play! *Plaaaaay*time!"

"Can't," Nathan informed him.

"Me either," said David.

"Why not? What else do you guys have to do?" Martin wanted to know.

"Homework!" they both told him.

"We have math, science, spelling . . . ," Nathan said.

". . . and reading. We have to read for twenty minutes," David added.

"Guys, are you feeling okay? Where'd this sudden sense of responsibility come from?" Martin asked.

"After what happened with the election speeches, we figure we gotta pay more attention to our work," Nathan said.

David nodded in agreement, adding, "We can play after."

"*Nooooooo!*" whined Martin. "I wanna play *now*!"

"Not now!" the boys said together.

Martin whined. A lot.

The boys ignored Martin and began unpacking their backpacks.

Then Martin slumped down on the couch and turned on the TV. "You're no fun at all!" he moaned.

But then he cheered up when his favorite show on the Challenge Channel—*So You Think*

You Can Beat This?—appeared. He made the TV louder. And louder. And louder.

"Record yourself setting a world record and you could win five thousand dollars!" the host boomed.

"Did you hear that?" Martin exclaimed.

"They heard it in Kansas," Nathan said, though no one could hear him.

"Turn it DOWN!" David screamed even louder   than the TV host was talking. "We are trying to do our homework!"

So Martin hit the mute button.

"Men, five thousand dollars could

put you both through college and buy you each sports cars and HDTVs!" he cried.

"No it couldn't," Nathan informed him.

"Not even close," said David.

"Okay, you're right. Then I'll keep all of the dough. The important thing is that we win, right?"

"Today's not exactly our day for winning," said David.

"Kid, this time victory is so close I can smell it. I can touch it. I can hear it. I can see it. And I can . . . wait—smell, touch, hear, see . . . um, um, um . . . ," Martin said, trying to figure out the fifth of the five senses.

"Taste it," Nathan offered.

"No thanks, I just had a ton of cookies," Martin said, totally missing the point.

Next, Martin ran to his room and returned with a video camera on a tripod. He scurried around to set it up.

"I won this sweet video setup on *America's Fuzziest Videos*," Martin said.

"You mean *Funniest*, right?" David asked.

"Oh, no," said Martin. "There was a prize for fuzziest video. And I won!" Then he lowered his voice. "I covered the camera lens with underwear."

Then Martin hit the record button, stepped back, and began addressing the camera. . . .

CHAPTER
SEVENTEEN

"Hello to all of my television fans, this is Martin Healey Discount, TABASCO extraordinaire, and the caretaker of Nathan and David Wohlfardt—don't worry, I'm working on a new last name for them—and we're here to set a world record and win that five thousand dollars. As you know or could probably guess, I am the world record holder for cross-country crawling. I've also high-fived everyone in Rhode Island, caught seven thousand, seven hundred and seventy-seven fish in four minutes with my teeth, and read every book—except one—in the Cleveland Public Library.

"And now . . . my greatest feat! Right before your eyes, these boys and I will set the international record for . . ."

The boys moved closer to hear.

". . . tossing a ball back and forth. The current record is twenty-three thousand, seven hundred and twenty-three times, set by two people named Schmutz and Schmear in a town so far outside Cleveland that it's actually in Texas. And the Virginia record is just over nine thousand. Here goes!"

Martin then tossed Nathan's ball to David, who continued to do his schoolwork as he tossed it to Nathan, who continued to do his schoolwork as he tossed it to Martin, who tossed it to David, and so on and so on. Martin counted the tosses and catches by fives, so it would go faster.

And when they reached ten thousand con-
secutive catches—having broken the state
record and a lamp, two picture frames, and a
wicker thing—Martin dashed into the kitchen
to see how much whipped cream he could
spray into his mouth in sixty seconds (not to
achieve a world record—he just liked whipped
cream). Then he came back in time to rejoin
the boys in the toss for the record.

When they reached 23,724 throws,
Martin called the TV station to claim the
five-thousand-dollar prize. But unfortunately,
he had been watching a very old episode that
was being rerun, and the cash prize had been
given away in 1975.

Also unfortunately, the living room looked
like a war zone. And Mr. and Mrs. Wohlfardt
would soon be home.

"Men, according to the time on my always
precise Time-Up watch—personally handed to

me by the presid—er, gover—er, mayor—er, salesclerk—you have exactly nineteen minutes to glue, paint, undent, and generally fix this extremely probably unfixable mess."

"*Us?* Why us?" David asked. "It was your idea. Your ball. Your world record . . ."

But Martin had left the room. The building. And maybe even the town. So the boys sprang into action. In a great panic, they glued and swept and wiped and stapled like mad.

There was so much to be done. And when Nathan checked the living room clock, the big hand was on the twelve and the little hand was on the floor, which meant . . . doom.

Martin returned to the scene when they had just a minute left to clean up the mess. He clapped his hands three times, stomped his left foot twice, pulled on both earlobes, and said, "*Plazinka!*" forty-three times.

What did repeatedly saying *"Plazinka!"* have to do with cleaning up the place in a hurry? Absolutely nothing. See, while he was stomping and pulling his earlobes and repeating that ridiculous word, Nathan and David got the whole job done. Everything was neat and tidy and orderly by the time Mrs. Wohlfardt put her key in the front door and walked inside.

"Mrs. Wohlfardt, welcome back to the Wohlfardt residence," Martin rushed to tell her.

"Why, thank you, Martin." Mrs. Wohlfardt smiled.

"Oh, dear Mrs. W, how I wish that there were a rewind button on the remote control of life," Martin said. "If there were, I could go back in time and show you two boys who did their homework immediately upon returning home from school!"

"Wonderful," Mrs. Wohlfardt said as she took a seat in a nearby easy chair. "Please do rewind and show me that, Martin."

Martin shook his head. "Alas, I cannot," he informed her. "But I can have the boys demonstrate their newfound skill of reciting the fives table up to seventeen thousand. Master Nathan, would you start?"

"Five," Nathan said with little emotion.

Mrs. Wohlfardt applauded wildly.

"Your turn, Master David," Martin urged.

"Ten," David said with little emotion.

Mrs. Wohlfardt applauded wildly once again.

"Fifteen," said Nathan, yawning.

Mrs. Wohlfardt applauded wildly once again, again.

"Perhaps you might want to hold your applause until they hit seventeen thousand, Mrs. Wohlfardt," Martin suggested. "I wouldn't want to have your hands peel, get irritated, or fall off."

Mrs. Wohlfardt thought that was an excellent idea, and she just watched and listened as the boys took turns saying numbers until David finally rasped, "Seventeen thousand."

Upon hearing that, Mrs. Wohlfardt leaped up on her chair, waved her arms, and exclaimed, "Genius! Pure genius!"

"Thanks, Mom," croaked David.

"Yeah. Thanks, Mom," croaked Nathan.

"I meant Martin," Mrs. Wohlfardt said. "But you boys did well too. Now run along, so I can continue telling Martin what a sensational job he's doing around here."

The boys left the room, once again feeling somewhat tricked by Martin. After all, they were the ones who did the counting, but Martin got the credit. They were the ones with a reputation for making a mess, but somehow, they ended up being the ones who had to take responsibility for doing the cleaning.

Like brushing their teeth at 10:30 a.m. . . . or doing their homework right after getting home from school . . . the counting and the cleaning up and the working on the same side made Nathan and David feel, well, different than they'd ever felt. It wasn't a *bad* feeling, really, but one that made them think about themselves and each other and their parents and their former nannies and (especially) their current nanny.

And then there was the matter of the ski trip hanging over their heads. It was complicated, to be sure, but if they failed or if Martin failed or if they failed to make Martin seem like he wasn't failing when in truth he failed at almost everything . . . they'd fail to go on the ski trip.

Why was the ski trip so important to them? Because it was a special getaway that they'd had every year since they could both remember. And when you've had something that long, you'll do everything you can to keep it. Even if that "everything" involves all they'd been forced to do since the day The Mustache took over.

The family feasted on delicious meat loaf that night. But the boys were too stressed out from the close-call, emergency cleanup to notice that the loaf seemed to be shaped oddly like Martin's head. They were so stressed out that music-hating Nathan sang throughout the meal, and David ate all the vegetables on the table, then asked for seconds and thirds. Now *that's* stressed.

CHAPTER
EIGHTEEN

Martin, too, had been stressed out lately. Although Mr. and Mrs. Wohlfardt hadn't asked to see his recommendation letters in a while, he knew that it was only a matter of time before one of them brought up the subject again.

Martin awoke with a start one night at precisely 3:17 a.m. He knew it was 3:17 a.m. because his alarm clock read 11:17 a.m., and Martin liked to keep his clock set to eight hours ahead so he always felt as if he had an extra one-third of a day more to have fun.

Knowing that the members of the Wohlfardt family were fast asleep (though not quite sure where the expression "fast asleep" came from, because truly, no one was doing anything fast while sleeping), Martin spoke softly to himself, weighing the possibilities.

"If Mr. Wohlfardt says, 'Martin, I'd like to see your recommendation letters,' or Mrs. Wohlfardt says, 'I'd like to see your recommendation letters, Martin' . . ."

(Mrs. Wohlfardt still hadn't broken the habit of ending every sentence with "Martin," which wasn't so bad when she was talking to him, but was utterly confusing when she said that at work and the person to whom she was speaking was named Rose or Simone.)

"What, oh what do I do? I could lie and tell them that they were destroyed in a tragic letter-of-recommendation accident, but that would be like lying, and I've heard that's not good.

"I could lie and tell them that I don't have them and I never had them, but that would be the truth and it wouldn't be lying at all, which would be good, but would be bad because then they'd know I don't have them and that I'd *never* had them.

"I could write some letters and sign them and show them to them, telling them that they were from the people who wrote them and signed them, making them think they were from them and not from me. . . ."

Martin repeated that last idea several times, simply because all the "thems" totally confused him.

"Or . . . I could fall asleep and dream an answer to this rather sticky, rather tricky problem."

And that's exactly what Martin did. He fell asleep within seconds, and dreamed that when he woke up, there'd be a pile of enthusiastic recommendation letters on his bed.

And guess what? When Martin woke up after a sound sleep and a happy dream, there were no recommendation letters by his side.

So, faced with having to tell the truth, having to admit he didn't actually have a single recommendation letter . . .

Martin turned over and went back to sleep.

"Martin," Mr. Wohlfardt said, "you have made such a difference in our home, and with our boys, that we've decided it would be ridiculous to ask you for letters of recommendation."

"I agree, Martin," said Mrs. Wohlfardt. "Your actions in this home are all the recommendation we need . . . ," she added.

Martin smiled, then paused, waiting for Mrs. Wohlfardt to finish speaking.

". . . Martin," she added.

Martin was overwhelmed with relief. He thought he was going to cry. And then . . .

Martin woke up again.

He looked around his bed for Mr. and Mrs. Wohlfardt. (They weren't there, of course.)

He looked around the room for the recommendation letters from his earlier dream. (They weren't there either, of course.)

Martin had dreamed a happy solution to his problem. But sadly, it was only a dream; he still had the problem.

So, faced with having to tell the truth, having to admit he didn't actually have a single recommendation letter, faced with not being excused from showing the letters by Mr. and Mrs. Wohlfardt . . .

Martin ripped a sheet of paper from his personal, double-secret, never-written-in diary and wrote down some of his best, most unique characteristics. While they weren't recommendations, to be sure they were reasons to admire Martin:

- Martin grew up with five brothers and two sisters, and slept in an octuple bunk bed. Martin was sixth from the bottom. He fell out of bed once a week, but strangely, never on a Thursday night.

- Martin remembers the lyrics to every song he's ever heard, but never recalls the melody. That's why he usually sings "Jingle Bells" to the tune of "The Star-Spangled Banner."

- Martin has had the same bar of shower soap since age ten, and it's never gotten any smaller. And despite what you might think, that isn't because Martin doesn't actually <u>use</u> the soap.

- Martin has a total of ten toes, but not always five on each foot.

- Martin tried out to play for his favorite baseball team, the Kansas City Royals, but he didn't actually hit the ball in more than one hundred at-bats, and didn't catch any of the ground balls or pop flies they hit his way. None of the pitches he threw came within twenty feet of home plate. The team asked him never to come to tryouts again. And, in fact, they requested that he root for another team entirely.

- In his spare time, Martin is an amateur tree surgeon.
- Martin has never given anyone change for a quarter, and hopes no one will ever ask him to do so.
- Martin is a fourteen-time department-store escalator-racing champion.
- Martin laughs every day at exactly 4:13 p.m.—even if there's nothing funny going on.

Martin reviewed the list for spelling and punctuation. Satisfied that it was well written and revealed his true nature, he then ripped it up, turned over, and went back to sleep.

CHAPTER
NINETEEN

It took all of David's holiday money, and some of his birthday money, and a few dollars of Nathan's emergency cash (*shh, don't tell Nathan*) . . . but David was confident that the Super-Sleuth Detective Kit was well worth it.

David was huddled in a dark corner of the basement, flashlight held between his teeth, studying the many pieces of the kit. He had all he needed to check hair follicles, analyze fingerprints, study DNA samples, investigate crime scene clues, decode secret messages, and out-spy a spy in many sneaky, tricky, clever, and sinister ways.

"Martin Healey Discount, prepare to be exposed as an international spy," David said, adding a not-so-sinister laugh, "Nyah-ha-haaaa!"

Gotta work on that laugh, he told himself.

Then, armed with the contents of the spy kit, David scampered around the house. He tiptoed through hallways, peered around corners, and moved through the house in a very spylike manner. From time to time, he stopped to collect loose strands of hair, lift fingerprints, and record important clues in his Official Secret Spy Notebook (which, come to think of it, shouldn't really have that written on it in big, bold letters, should it?).

When David got to Martin's bedroom door, he wrote the following in his notebook:

11:03 a.m. in the morning.

SIS (Suspected International Spy) is in the garden, picking tomatoes for his tomato and tomato sandwiches (don't ask).

Door is locked.

Will lift DNA from the doorknob.

Strange buzzing from behind the door.

No one has seen the contents of this room since the SIS moved in. Will try to gain access through spy methods or surprise politeness.

Plan to check hair samples, finger-prints, and DNA, and review clues to further determine if SIS is an AIS (Actual International Spy).

Time for a snack.

After his snack (hey, a spy tracker's gotta eat), David used his kit to analyze the samples he'd collected. And after studying and matching them to the handbook from the kit, he was convinced that the samples came from a 104-year-old woman from Tibet. Or a three-day-old baby. Neither of which had ever been in the Wohlfardt house (at least since David and Nathan had been three-day-old babies).

"Back to the drawing board," David sighed, knowing full well that his family didn't actually own a drawing board. "But I'll *prove* that Martin Healey Discount is an international spy, or my name isn't . . . isn't . . . isn't . . . X-14-Double L-7."

(Which, in fact, it *wasn't*.)

CHAPTER TWENTY

Of all the boring afternoons in a lifetime of occasionally boring days, Saturday, October 5, had to be the boringest ever. David stared at Nathan. Nathan stared at David. And Martin, who was very vain, stared at himself in the mirror. He smiled. He smirked. He struck poses. Usually he found this utterly fascinating. But not today.

There was absolutely nothing interesting to do.

David sighed.

Nathan sighed.

Martin sighed.

"I can't think of a single thing to do," David said.

"Me either," Nathan said.

"Why don't you boys pick up your backpacks and do some studying?" Martin suggested.

"Good one, Martin," Nathan said. "But Mom and Dad aren't around, so you don't have to suggest things that make us do work."

"Yeah," David agreed. "Save those bothersome ideas for when our parents are around so you get credit for being a genius nanny when we all know the real . . ."

David paused. ". . . um, er, I, that is . . ."

Martin raised an eyebrow. "The real . . . ?" he wanted to know. "The real *what*?"

David realized he had nearly insulted Martin.

"The real *Mona Lisa* painting is worth a fortune, though there have been many copies," David said, changing subjects. "We read about that in art."

Either the nanny hadn't actually been insulted, or he quickly forgave David, because Martin immediately went back to being bored.

"I wish this family had a pet we could play with," Martin whined.

The boys both got a little interested. "But Mom's allergic to anything with fur," David said. "So we can never have a pet in the house."

"It's so unfair!" Martin said as he pounded a couch pillow in frustration. "Why me? Why me? Why *meeeee*?" He frowned. But soon his frown turned into a smile. Then he bolted upright. "I have it!" Martin yelled excitedly.

Nathan and David both looked at Martin as he continued.

"I can solve the pet problem *and* the allergy problem! What this house needs is an East Dakotan hairless mini hyena!"

The boys stared at Martin as he giggled and somersaulted all the way out the door.

Then he dashed back in and said, "Don't tell your mother or father I left you alone. I'll be back before you can say . . ."

And with that, Martin ducked out the door and was gone again.

"Before we can say what?" David wondered.

"Before we can say, 'We're alone. Just us in the house. No one to tell us what to do or not to do,'" Nathan said.

"Hey, yeah! This is the moment we've always dreamed of," David told him. "We can eat whatever we want. We can do whatever we want. We can watch whatever we want. After we make a pact to not tell on each other, what should we do wrong first?"

"You know, bro?" Nathan said. "I don't really want to do anything we shouldn't just 'cause there's no adult around."

"What, are you getting *mature* or something?" David wanted to know.

"Nah. Well, I dunno," Nathan told him. "It just feels wrong to do wrong things just for the sake of doing them."

David suddenly realized he agreed, but he didn't have a chance to respond. Because right then, Martin came hopping back into the house with the smallest, cutest, un-furriest creature the boys had ever seen!

"Men, meet Half Nelson, a real-life hairless mini hyena from Phlegmalia! He's playful, cute, and best of all, he's one hundred percent hypoallergenic! That means no wheeze, no sneeze, and by the way, no fleas!"

Nathan and David were thrilled (and to be sure, Mr. Wohlfardt would have enjoyed the triple rhyme). They petted him. They cooed over him. They took turns holding him.

But the moment the icemaker in the kitchen freezer let out an ice-dumping thud, Half Nelson was startled. He sprang out of their arms and raced around and around the house, laughing like a hyena. (After all, he *was* a hyena. Well, a mini one.) The boys chased him but couldn't catch him. Then they found him next to the refrigerator, gulping down raw sirloin steaks—two at a time!

As they grabbed for him, he took off, charged around the house laughing, then disappeared. The boys spent all afternoon looking for Half Nelson.

Martin had indeed solved the boredom problem and the pet problem. But now there was a bigger problem. There was a wild hyena loose in the house!

Just then, Mrs. Wohlfardt walked in.

"Achoo!"

"Achoo! Achoo!"

"Achoo! Achoo! Achoo!"

"Achoo! Achoo! Achoo! Achoo!"

"Achoo! Achoo! Achoo! Achoo! Achoo!"

"Achoo! Achoo! Achoo! Achoo! Achoo! Achoo!"

"Hear that, men? The sound of a twenty-one-sneeze salute!"

*"A-a-a-a—*Is there a dog in this house?—*choo!"* Mrs. Wohlfardt demanded.

"Mrs. Wohlfardt, knowing how allergic you are, I'd never allow these fine young lads to bring a dog on the premises," Martin assured her. "But guess again."

"Achoo! A cat?"

"Certainly not. Any other ideas?"

"Achoo! A hamster?"

"No."

"Achoo! A gerbil? Raccoon? Snake?"

"No. No. And blech, no."

Nathan and David knew that it would probably take a couple of weeks for their mother to get around to guessing it was a hairless mini hyena from Phlegmalia. But they also knew they had to find Half Nelson. Now!

As the boys scurried around the room repeatedly bashing into each other, Martin turned the house upside down looking for Half Nelson.

That's not a figure of speech. He literally turned the house upside down. And at last, Half Nelson popped out of Mr. Wohlfardt's golf bag. The hairless mini hyena had fallen madly in love with the fluffy cover on Mr. Wohlfardt's nine-iron.

Martin scolded Half Nelson for running away. He also scolded him for causing Mrs. Wohlfardt's allergic reaction. "You're supposed to be one hundred percent hypoallergenic, you silly hyena!"

Half Nelson was insulted. He shed a tear while letting out a loud hyena laugh, then

Martin swooped him up and dashed out the door to transport Half Nelson to Kalamazoo, Michigan, where Martin had a cousin who owned a decorate-your-own-pottery shop.

Meanwhile, the boys spent the rest of the day scrubbing down the entire house to get rid of all traces of the mini hyena. After that, exhausted and with little time to do anything else, Nathan and David grabbed their backpacks and began studying.

When the house was de-Half-Nelsoned and Mrs. Wohlfardt had stopped sneezing, Martin explained to her that it must have been the men's aftershave sample from his current issue of *Sensational Nanny Monthly* that he'd used that caused her allergic reaction.

Totally unaware of the commotion, Mrs. Wohlfardt commended Martin for his extreme honesty and thoughtfulness, and even offered to buy him a lifetime subscription to that magazine (which would be extremely hard to do, since it doesn't actually exist).

"Martin," Mrs. Wohlfardt added, now seemingly in the habit of starting *and* ending every sentence with the nanny's name, "you have changed my boys' lives. They are cleaning. They are studying. They are all-around solid citizens . . . when they used to be seen as, well, liquid citizens, Martin."

"I know exactly what you mean," Martin told her, though clearly he didn't. No one could possibly have known what she meant.

And no one could possibly have predicted that she'd think Martin was the greatest nanny ever, ever, ever. But that's what she said. Well, actually, she said, "Martin, you're the greatest nanny ever, ever, ever, Martin."

And don't bother looking up "liquid citizen." There's no such thing.

CHAPTER
TWENTY-ONE

Martin had been a member of the Wohlfardt household for forty-two days, nine hours, and six minutes, and though they still hadn't seen his letters of recommendation, Mr. and Mrs. Wohlfardt still absolutely adored him.

So life was pretty good for Martin, except for one thing that kept him feeling edgy. It was the conversation he accidentally overheard while standing with his ear pressed against Nathan and David's bedroom door:

"Hey, Nathan, if we do get to go on the trip, do you think Mom and Dad will invite Martin?" David asked.

"I dunno, maybe," Nathan answered. "Sometimes they ask the nannies to come with us, sometimes they don't."

Martin walked away after that, and never heard what the boys said next:

"I hope Martin *is* invited," said Nathan.

"Me too," said David. "Even if it might mean that he'd make us alphabetize the ski slope or something like that."

But having walked away, Martin never heard those words. Instead, the two things he took away from the eavesdropping were a flattened ear and a sense that the Wohlfardts didn't really consider him a member of the family. But if other nannies had earned their way onto family trips, that's what *he* wanted too! After all, he was *very* competitive.

Which is exactly why soon after, Martin quizzed the boys as he did some self-created yoga moves on the kitchen table.

"You've had three hundred and forty-seven nannies?" he asked.

"Or seven hundred and thirty-four," David said as he tried to eat breakfast while ducking Martin's crisscrossed feet. "We're not sure."

Martin's mustache twitched. "And I'm the best, right?" he asked.

"You're not the worst," Nathan said, looking up from a steaming bowl of oatmeal, which is something that no previous nanny had ever been able to convince him to try. But since Martin had tricked him into eating it, Nathan found he loved it. Absolutely loved it.

"I'd say . . . definitely in the top one hundred and seventeen," added David.

Somehow that brought out Martin's spirited side; he suddenly wanted to be their Best Nanny Ever (as long as it didn't take a lick of actual extra work, of course).

After all, being crowned Best Nanny Ever would surely take Martin off the hook regarding the letters of recommendation.

And that's when he decided he simply had to learn all the best-loved secrets of the other nannies—to absolutely guarantee that he was the best of all. So he snuck into the next room, picked up the phone, zipped through the Wohlfardt speed dial, and made some calls.

"Wohlfardt? No!" screamed one voice after another on the phone. One person Martin dialed even had an outgoing answering machine message that said, "Please leave a message at the beep, unless you're calling from 82727294 Flerch Street in Screamersville. In that case, please hang up and lose this phone number. Thank you, and have a wonderful day."

But Martin managed to keep quite a few nannies on the phone long enough to invite them. (He told one she'd won the lottery, another that she'd won a car, and yet another that she'd won Minnesota.) He copied down their favorite recipes. And . . . since Mr. and Mrs. Wohlfardt were planning to be out that evening, he invited each of the nannies to a "Teach Martin" surprise reunion dinner.

It was a perfect plan. Soon Martin would be the Babysitter of the Universe!

Martin was sure Mr. and Mrs. Wohlfardt would leave the house promptly at six; he knew they didn't want to miss a moment of the annual Parents Who Attend Too Many Dinners dinner at the boys' school. And indeed, they left at 5:59—which gave Martin just enough time to try to read all his recipe notes and prepare the most special dinner ever. Or perhaps the second-most special. Or the 928th.

Moments later, as the boys sat down at the table, the doorbell rang.

"Oh, who could that be?" Martin asked, knowing full well that it was Maria or Maria or Maria or Maria or Maria or Maria or Maria or Ibi.

It turned out to be Maria. And soon after, Maria rang the bell. Then Maria. Then Ibi. And to make a long story short, there were soon two Wohlfardts hugging eight former nannies, followed by eight former nannies hugging Martin. (The eight former nannies didn't hug one another because, in fact, they'd never met one another.)

After the massive hugging session, they all sat down to a dinner that Martin had prepared based on all the nannies' favorite recipes. Did he succeed? Well, as the fourth Maria said, it was simply . . .

LUFWA.

Inedible, really. The meatballs tasted like melon. The melon tasted like mothballs. The mothballs tasted like egg salad (they were pretty good, actually, but no one knew it, 'cause who wants to eat mothballs?). And the soup tasted like armpit. (Left armpit, to be specific. Right armpit tastes kind of sweet and tangy, while left armpit is usually salty and quite . . . oh, never mind.)

The second Maria asked for seconds. The third Maria asked for thirds. The fourth Maria almost threw up.

At one point, David passed the candied yams to Ibi, who used them to give herself a relaxing facial massage. And when the sixth Maria saw that, she realized that Ibi was her long-lost sister. They embraced, cried, and performed their native Majma-Flajma dance on the dining room table.

The whole night was a lot of bad food and noise and confusion. The horrible cooking also gave the house a foul odor that you could actually see. Everyone was holding their noses and keeping their mouths tightly shut, which definitely made it hard to eat pork à la bananas flambé with hot-fudge gravy. Thinking quickly, Martin grabbed the family's Truman 6000 Airvac (the vac with the sales pitch "This is the vacuum to use, because you spell 'vacuum' with two 'U's!"), and he swung it around wildly to suck up the odor. It also snatched

the fifth Maria's wig, the first Maria's necklace, and . . . the third Maria's homemade name badge that said *I Wish I'd Been the Second Maria.*

At precisely 10:04 p.m., Martin suddenly announced that it was time for the nannies to go home. But just as they all scrambled for their coats and lined up to leave, the front door swung open and Mr. and Mrs. Wohlfardt entered.

"We are ho—" Mrs. Wohlfardt.

"Welcome ho!" shouted Martin, trying to block the fact that he'd filled the house with a houseful of former nannies.

Mr. and Mrs. Wohlfardt stepped around Martin; they couldn't believe the crowd, the smell, or the insane mess in the kitchen. Nathan and David felt sure that their parents were going to yell at Martin for causing such chaos on a school night.

Once the nannies had noisily filed out, Martin made a deeply heartfelt, deeply moving, and deeply nonsensical speech:

"Mr. and Mrs. Wohlfardt, I'm sure you want an explanation. Well, that is, you see, your young men are so special to me that I simply could not bear the thought of them tearfully missing their once-beloved former nannies. And so, I went to great lengths to learn their most special recipes, best bedtime stories, and most family-pleasing tips. That's what this was all about. And did it leave a smell? Yes. A leftover kitchen mess? Perhaps. But it's a smell of caring . . . and a mess of love!"

Mrs. Wohlfardt started crying. Mr. Wohlfardt looked like he might too.

Nathan and David just slapped their foreheads. *The Mustache* had somehow managed to do something bad and come out looking good, and their parents were thrilled, just thrilled, that Martin cared enough about the family to try to become as wonderful as all the other nannies put together.

Mr. and Mrs. Wohlfardt ignored the fact that he hadn't actually learned a single thing from any of the Marias or Ibi (or any of the other nannies he'd spoken to).

Mrs. Wohlfardt called Martin "the nanny of the century. In fact, the nanny of *last* century too! Truly one in a million, Martin."

David rolled his eyes and said to Nathan, "He is one in a million. The *worst* one in a million. Why couldn't Mom have hired any of the other nine hundred ninety-nine thousand, nine hundred ninety-nine nannies?"

"And why didn't *Blerblemowcha* show up for the reunion?" asked Nathan.

The night ended happily (if you don't count the fact that the second Maria thought the

Wohlfardts' car was her prize and drove off in it, or that the third Maria now thinks she owns Minnesota. Or that Ibi's face smelled like candied yams for months afterward.).

Mrs. Wohlfardt decided that in honor of Martin's extra-special display of affection for the family, they would hold a small ceremony. Mr. Wohlfardt had the boys fetch the Nanny-o-Meter™ and give it to Martin. They also had David rejigger it so it was permanently set to '1'—to signify that there was only one nanny in the Wohlfardts' lives, now and forevermore.

Even though the Nanny-o-Meter™ was falling apart, it was quite a remarkable trophy for the Best Nanny Ever to receive.

Martin claimed he was totally unprepared for this wonderful recognition, then made a twenty-seven-minute speech in which he thanked everyone he'd ever met (except, strangely, any members of the Wohlfardt family), kissed every piece of furniture in the living room, and cried until there was an actual puddle at his feet (which the boys were told to mop up, of course).

Good night.

CHAPTER
TWENTY-TWO

"We need a new basketball hoop," David complained one day as he shot the ball and watched it roll off their rusty hoop. The hoop was so bent that the ball would not go all the way through.

"If you need new sporting equipment, my good fellows," Martin said loudly as Mr. and Mrs. Wohlfardt passed by on their way to the car, "you should earn the funding yourselves. After all, there is pride in a job well done, not a gift well gifted."

Nathan and David couldn't believe their ears. Earn their own money? *Them?*

"That's a splendid idea," Mrs. Wohlfardt said as she got into the car. "Martin is right—if you boys earn the money for the hoop, you'll enjoy it more!"

As Mr. and Mrs. Wohlfardt drove away, Martin winked at the boys.

"Don't worry," he said. "I'm gonna help you out."

The boys gulped.

"Are you going to buy us a hoop?" Nathan asked.

"No," said Martin. "But I'll help you raise the cash."

"How?" asked David.

"How?" said Martin. "How? I happen to be the Chancellor of Lemonade, that's how. And I'll even share my ultra-secret family juicing recipe, which was passed down by my ultra-secret family."

Moments later, Martin invaded the Wohl-fardts' kitchen and emerged with a pitcher of his "famous" lemonade. Then the trio headed out to build their stand and to seek fame and fortune as lemonade sellers. David set up the table and cash box. And Nathan carried the pitcher of lemonade and a package of cups out of the house.

Martin carried nothing—that is, nothing but a huge plastic garbage bag.

When all was set up, Martin opened the garbage bag and pulled out a padded chaise longue and a giant flashing neon sign that read:

FREE world-class lemonade—only 47¢

Then Martin promptly took a nap while the boys worked.

As soon as the first customer took a single sip, word spread throughout the neighborhood.

In no time at all, there was a line halfway down the block, and in the first ten minutes, they had raised $78.02.

Martin sent the boys back inside for more lemonade. Then he sent them back for more cups. David ran in to use the bathroom, because he had personally drunk $26.32 worth of lemonade. And Martin ran in for more food.

Sales mounted. On Martin's fifth trip back for more food, he brought along a batch of his ultra-secret cookies, passed down by the same ultra-secret family.

Later in the day, Martin added his super-double-ultra-secret brownies to the menu. Then his never-before-served sandwiches. His dandy candy apples. And finally . . . Aunt Marvin's legendary chicken fricassee.

By sundown, they'd sold more than five hundred dollars' worth of food and drinks. David was tired. Nathan was wiped out. And Martin was sore from lying on his chaise longue all day. His sunburn hurt a little too.

But Nathan and David were ecstatic. As they walked home with Martin, the boys realized they'd earned enough for the basketball hoop *and* some hockey equipment.

"Look at all this money!" Nathan declared. "We're rich!"

"I wonder how much you need to be a millionaire," David asked.

Obviously, Nathan didn't answer the obvious question. When they got inside the house, the boys found the cupboards were bare. The fridge was completely empty. Why, it looked as if someone had ransacked the kitchen.

And indeed, someone had.

Unfortunately, what they'd sold all day was food that Martin had taken from the Wohlfardts' pantry. No, there were no secret family recipes. Martin had pretty much sold off everything in sight (except for a turkey leg on the counter, which he picked up and nibbled on).

"Someone's been eating in our house," David said.

"Good guess, Goldilocks!" Nathan laughed. "Martin, you cleaned this place out!"

What a problem. What to do? It was dinnertime, and there was nothing to eat in the house, save the old salami sandwich under Nathan's bed (or was it peanut butter?) that now looked more like a science experiment. How would Martin squirm out of this one? Would the Wohlfardt parents finally discover the real Martin?

Not a chance.

Martin marched the boys into the den to explain the whole business to Mr. and Mrs. Wohlfardt.

"Why, I've taught your boys the lesson of a lifetime—responsible business!"

He showed Mr. and Mrs. Wohlfardt all the money that Nathan and David had made at the lemonade stand. Then he explained how much they owed for the food and drinks taken from the Wohlfardt kitchen.

"And," Martin continued, "the remaining profit—ten dollars—will go to charity."

"We're so proud of our boys!" Mr. Wohlfardt exclaimed.

"Martin, all three of you make quite a team!" Mrs. Wohlfardt agreed. "Thank you, Martin!"

Then Mr. and Mrs. Wohlfardt went out for dinner to celebrate their responsible family (and also to celebrate the seven thousandth day since their first date).

As for Martin and the boys, they went on a huge food shopping expedition to the biggest supermarket in town.

So when Mr. and Mrs. W got home from their dinner later, the cupboards and fridge were fully restocked. They were so thrilled—"Oh, thank you, Martin!" Mrs. Wohlfardt said again—they went out for coffee to continue celebrating their joyous family (and also to celebrate that it had been one hour since their dinner to celebrate the seven thousandth day since their first date—

the Wohlfardts were a very sentimental couple).

Once again, the boys had done almost all the work and gotten pretty much none of the credit. Nathan and David knew that their lives were changing because of this strange, unusual (possible spy) nanny. And no matter how much they thought about it, they couldn't decide if Martin Healey Discount was the best thing ever to happen to them . . . or the worst.

They'd soon know for sure.

Or would they?

CHAPTER
TWENTY-THREE

It had been nearly six months since The Mustache had taken over at the Wohlfardt household. And while kids regularly get report cards at school, they don't usually receive them based on their behavior at home. But if Nathan and David sat down and looked at their lives and thought about how they'd changed under Martin's "care," the grades they'd give to themselves would be pretty eye-opening.

Their grade for getting along, which would have been an F prior to knowing Martin, would be a B-plus.

The only thing keeping them from an A was the time that Nathan ate David's last dried fruit snack, so David put pudding in Nathan's best dress shoes, so Nathan served David that pudding as a snack, so David walked around with the taste of chocolate-covered feet in his mouth, so he put Styrofoam peanuts from a package they'd received into his brother's lunch box and Nathan ate them, thinking they were some kind of new potato-y snack.

Please don't do any of that, but all those things made for quite a fight between the boys, and that's why they wouldn't get an A.

Their grade for cleanliness, which would have been a triple F-minus prior to knowing Martin, would be an A. See, because Martin showed off his leadership in front of their parents so often, the boys were forever cleaning, tidying, organizing, and vacuuming. In fact, if you were to find any clutter at all in their room, there's a pretty good chance it would have been alphabetized.

Their grade for dedication to their studies, which would have been a septuple F-double-minus prior to knowing Martin, was an A-minus. They studied. They did well on tests. They showed how smart they were, or, in a few cases, how smart they *weren't*. But they tried. Yes, they tried.

And finally, their grade for being good sons, for treating their parents with honor, respect, and courtesy, which would have been a C-plus prior to knowing Martin, would be an . . .

X.

Or a Y.

Or a Z.

Or a Z-minus-minus-minus-minus-minus. (Minus!)

See, Nathan and David had really improved in so many important ways. Ways that thrilled, thrilled, *thrilled* their parents. But . . .

Nathan and David realized that their mom and dad were too busy to notice (or too happy to care) that Martin wasn't really taking care of the boys . . . *the boys were taking care of him.*

Whenever he made a mess, they cleaned it up.

Whenever he broke something, they fixed it.

Whenever he did something wrong, they made it right.

They were only better because he was worse.

Which was never the case with Maria or Maria or Maria or Ibi. Or even Susan.

"I think it's time that Mom and Dad hear the truth about Martin," Nathan said. "I mean, he's a hoot, but he makes us do our own stuff, plus all the stuff it takes to make him look good."

"Yeah, I think they should know the whole story," David agreed. "Maybe they can get him to change . . . even a little. . . ."

Nathan and David realized it was the first time they had ever worked together willingly on a single task. It felt good, but it also felt strange. And it lasted only a few seconds, until David said, "What do you think you'll say to them?"

"*Me?* Why me?" Nathan wanted to know.

"Okay, *us* then," David agreed, not wanting to fight (and *wow*, did that feel strange too).

The boys worked on what they'd tell their parents.

"We'll say that Martin has acted one way in front of Mom and Dad, but a whole different way when they aren't around," said David.

"We'll say that Martin has been responsible for one mess after another, including the disgusting nanny dinner," said Nathan.

"We'll tell that Mom's incredible sneezing attack was caused by the mini hyena that Martin smuggled into the house."

"And we'll tell that neither one of us was elected school president because of Martin's ridiculous speeches."

"And we'll remind them that Martin has never actually shown them any letters of recommendation," said David.

"Um, Dave," Nathan said. "What if we tell Mom and Dad all this and they *fire* Martin?"

"They wouldn't do that," David said. "And don't call me Dave."

"They might fire him for real," Nathan argued. "After all, this is some pretty serious stuff."

"I don't think they'd fire him, Nath," David reassured his brother. "They'd just watch him a little closer, that's all."

"Don't call me Nath. And what happens to *us* if they watch him closer?" Nathan asked.

David didn't have an answer to that one.

"And . . . if they fire him and say it's our fault, we don't get the ski trip!" Nathan blurted out.

"And then if they hire someone new, it could be someone even worse!" David said.

"Could happen."

Suddenly the boys were confused. They didn't know whether to keep things as crazy as they were, or risk losing Martin and the ski trip and maybe end up with an even ninnier nanny.

Neither boy spoke for a while. Then David brightened and said, "Forget all that other anti-Martin stuff. We only have to tell Mom and Dad one thing. . . ."

"What's that?" Nathan asked.

"That we know for a fact, beyond a shadow of a doubt, that Martin Healey Discount is . . . a spy!"

CHAPTER
TWENTY-FOUR

Of course, thus far, David hadn't proved that Martin *was* a spy. He hadn't proved anything at all, really. So it was with little hope that he pulled out his kit to try another spy-catching mission.

But . . .

When he opened the box, everything in the kit was fully used up. There wasn't any more fingerprint-lifting stuff. No DNA-checking stuff. No hair sample gunk. And no secret-message-revealing thingies.

"What the heck?" he said aloud. "Now I have to buy another Super-Sleuth Detective Kit to find out who used the rest of my Super-Sleuth Detective Kit!"

"It's no mystery," said a squeaky voice.

"Stop that, Nathan," David said. "You're scaring me."

"That wasn't me," Nathan said. "The voice was coming from under the couch."

"H-hello?" David said in a hushed tone.

"H-hello, my friendy friends!" said Martin, sliding out from under the couch with his arms open to greet David and Nathan.

"Martin, did you use my Super-Sleuth Detective Kit?" David demanded.

"Maybe I did, and maybe I didn't," said Martin, adding a sinister *"Nyah-ha-haaaa!"*

"Ooh, that was a great sinister laugh," David said with tremendous admiration. "Can you teach that to me?"

Martin said he'd be glad to. But first, he wanted David to tell him something.

"Sure, Martin, anything," David said nervously.

"Why were you using this kit?" Martin wanted to know. "Did you think your brother was a spy?"

"Uh, no," David said.

"Did you think your mother was a spy?"

"Certainly not," David said.

"Did you think your father was a spy?"

"Not at all," David said.

"Not your brother. Not your mother. Not your father. So who's left? Huh? Who? Huh?

Huh? Who? Who? Huh? Who?" Martin said as he inched closer and closer and closer to David.

"Who?" David repeated, trying to buy time.

"Yes, who's left? Huh? Who? Huh? Huh? Who? Who? Huh? Who?"

"Well, the only two other people in the house are me . . . and"—*gulp*—"you," David said.

"Well, kid"—Martin glared—"I guess we solved this case after all, huh?"

"What do you mean, Martin?"

"You thought *I* was a spy, didn't you? You thought I was here on some kind of secret mission, plotting, scheming, dreaming, and bleaming, didn't you?"

"Bleaming?" David asked. "What's bleaming?"

"Wouldn't you like to know," Martin said. "Now admit it, you thought I was a spy."

David felt himself about to panic. Maybe even about to cry.

"Yes, Martin, I did," David said. "After all, you have to admit that you have rather unusual ways of doing things."

"I am one of a kind, to be sure. But is there anything wrong with that?" Martin said.

"Uh, no," David told him.

"Uh, no," Nathan agreed.

"My ways may be different, but they are effective," Martin told them. "After all, some spell a name 'J-E-A-N,' others spell it 'J-E-A-N-N-E,' and still others spell it 'G-E-N-E.' If that was my name, I'd spell it 'F-R-E-D.' Does that make me a bad person? I think not."

"Of course not," said David, who wasn't quite sure what they were talking about.

"And answer me this: out of all the nannies who came before me, did any of them help you and your brother stop fighting with each other and start being better students and more responsible kids?"

David thought about it and said, "No, Martin, just you."

"Indeed," said Martin. "Did any of them help you work harder and dream bigger?"

Nathan thought about it and said, "No, Martin, just you."

"Indeed," said Martin. "Did any of them help you discover the joys of new foods?"

David and Nathan thought about it and said, "No, Martin, just you."

"Indeed," said Martin. "Did any of them take you on a mini safari in Africa to find new species of elephants?"

David and Nathan thought about it and said, "No, Martin, but you didn't either."

"Well, I was planning to," Martin said. "I most certainly was planning to. But I did help you with all those other things, didn't I?"

"Yes, Martin," David said.

"Didn't I?"

"Yes, Martin," Nathan said.

"And for that I get suspected as a spy?"

"I'm sorry, Martin," David said. "Really, really sorry."

"Forget it, kid," Martin said. "I forgive you."

"Thanks, Martin." David brightened. "Thanks a lot."

Martin patted David on the back and turned to leave the room.

"Oh, one more thing," Martin called to David.

"Yes, Martin?"

"I *am* a spy. And according to that kit, your mother is too. And so's your father. *Nyah-ha-haaaa!*"

CHAPTER
TWENTY-FIVE

On the six-month anniversary of the day Martin first arrived at the Wohlfardts' door, he threw himself a half-year, half-day party. Half a cake. Half a scoop of ice cream. Even half a balloon.

And it was on that day that Martin invited the boys into his room for the first time. They had always been very curious about what was in there—but Martin had fourteen locks, three alarm systems, five security cameras, two remote-controlled guards, and a recording of a snarling German shepherd to keep them out.

Today, however, was different.

They entered the room that their nanny referred to as the Martin Lounge. The boys were captivated by his giant ice sculpture of a parrot, and his very own soda machine that sold only orange soda. And they were mesmerized by the motorized carousel in his room.

It was an exciting, enchanting place to visit, to be sure. David was very excited and a little enchanted to be there. Nathan was very enchanted and a little excited to be there. But their excitement and enchantment stopped when Martin said in a very serious tone, "Sit down, boys."

"Uh-oh," said David.

"Uh-oh," said Nathan.

"Why the 'uh-ohs,' gents?" Martin asked.

"Because every time a babysitter has told us to sit down, it was always followed by an 'I'm leaving,'" David said.

Nathan nodded in agreement.

"Well, guys," Martin said, "I'm leaving."

"That's not funny, Martin," Nathan said. "Not funny at all."

"Wasn't meant to be funny," Martin said. "The fact is, I am leaving. I'm heading out on the midnight train to . . . to . . ."

"Georgia?" David asked.

"Nope," said Martin. "Name's Martin. Haven't you remembered that by now?"

With that, Martin handed the boys a scroll and told them to run and show it

to their parents. They did, though they didn't run, because as they'd learned during Martin's recent In-House Kentucky Derby exercise program, it's not a good idea to run in the house.

Nathan and David found their parents in the master bedroom. And when Mr. Wohlfardt opened the scroll and read it aloud, both he and Mrs. Wohlfardt began to cry. The scroll read:

Dear Mr. and Mrs. Wohlfardt,

When I arrived at your home six months ago, I looked around and said to myself, "This is a place I could stay for five months. Or maybe five months and twenty-nine days." But I never, never, never expected to stay as long as six months.

During my time here, you have changed me. And I suspect I have changed you as well. And when I've changed you, you've found new ways to change me. And then I found other new ways to change you as well, and as a result, you changed me in even more ways. Which is to say we've changed each other, which is a good thing, because I believe we've all changed for the better, except for the time I thought I heard you ask me to boil your antique china plates in shampoo but you were really just saying, "Good morning, Martin, have a nice day" and I did the boiling thing and it was a disaster but I never told you, so I'm not going to tell you now.

When I arrived at your home, the boys were, well, immature poo-poo heads. They fought with each other. They were sloppy. They ate garbage. And they didn't care about schoolwork.

But guess what, Mr. and Mrs. Wohlfardt: I'm a bigger immature poo-poo head. I, too, fight with my twin brother, though I may not have one yet. I'm very sloppy as well. I eat garbage. And I can't do 50 percent of the work your boys do in school (though I might be pretty good at the other 70 percent).

Here's my whole deal: I pretended to be an all-star nanny with great experience, but really, I'm just a guy who likes to have fun. I really, really like your kids, and it's been a blast to be around them, but as you can tell by not reading the recommendation letters I never showed you, I am not a TABASCO, and I am certainly not a world-class nanny.

I am, instead, a world-class fraud.

But (and this is a big "but")... while I made you think I was a certified expert in childcare, the fact is, my laziness, my sloppiness, and my inattention to detail are what made your boys shape up and become solid citizens.

So while my time in your home has been full of madness, it's been madness with a tremendous lesson attached to it. And that lesson is: Don't Be Like Martin.

I didn't need a ton of bricks to fall on my head to realize that. And when the ton of bricks recently fell on my head, it really hurt. So now, I must leave at once.

Please do not try to contact me. Please do not call me or e-mail me or mail me or text me. Please do not wander the streets during the night yelling, "Martin, please come back!" because I won't be nearby to hear you, and if I am nearby, I won't come.

Remember that the smell of the joys of knowing me will always remain in the air throughout your home, and I hope you'll pick up a copy or two of my new book, which I plan to call <u>The Day the Mustache Took Over</u>.

The message had been puzzling, but that last line really confused everyone. They all scratched their heads in wonderment, and Nathan asked, "Hey, how come people scratch their heads when they're confused?"

Mr. Wohlfardt told him he didn't know, and anyway, he had to get back to Martin's message. He continued reading:

Dear Wohlfardts, I will think of you often. Well, at least often for me.

As for my future plans, I have a burning desire to become a used-car salesman in a country that begins with the letter "M." I won't tell you which one, but it's not Mexico or Morocco. Or France.

So long, y'all!

As the final sounds of "y'all" hung in the air, Mr. Wohlfardt looked at Nathan and David and said, "Boys, is this true? Was Martin less than perfect when your mom and I weren't around?"

David and Nathan told them yes, that was all true. But they took turns pointing out that it was also true that they *were* better in school, and better to each other, and just better—all because of Martin.

Nathan and David also told their parents that they feared their (well, mostly David's) "Martin is a spy" suspicions had offended Martin and prompted him to quit. They also said that they'd heard their mom and dad were spies, which Mr. and Mrs. Wohlfardt quickly denied, but not in a very convincing way. However, that was an issue for another time.

And the boys told their parents that they'd do anything to get Martin to stay. They said they didn't care about the ski trip—they just wanted Martin Healey Discount to remain *their* Martin Healey Discount.

Mr. Wohlfardt stomped his foot, thrust his arm in the air, and shouted, "This man is a fake. A fraud. A sham. A phony. But he's *our* fake, fraud, sham, and phony, and by golly, we must convince him that he belongs with the Wohlfardts!"

The family ran to Martin's room, where Mr. Wohlfardt reasoned with Martin. He begged Martin to stay. He pleaded. He offered him an increase in salary. He offered him the master bedroom. He offered him more vacation days. He even tried to bribe him with a car, a boat, and a pony. Martin raised an eyebrow at the mention of the pony.

Martin said, "Pardon me for a moment, won't you?" Then he backed into his bedroom and closed the door.

"Thinking it over!" Martin said from behind the door.

"Still thinking."

"Still thinking."

"*Still* thinking."

And then . . . silence.

The family waited quite a while for the door to open, but it never did.

"Are you still thinking?" Mr. Wohlfardt asked through the door.

"Please be still thinking, Martin," Mrs. Wohlfardt added, even though that wasn't totally grammatically correct.

After another short period of silence, Mr. Wohlfardt knocked on the door, and it swung open. That's when the family saw . . . the room was empty. One hundred percent empty, except for the Nanny-o-Meter™ lying on the floor. Nathan and David looked for the ice sculpture, soda machine, and carousel. All were gone. So were all of Martin's things, and even his bed.

Martin had ducked out through the window, and there was no sign that he had ever been there at all.

Nathan and David were instantly sad that their beloved nanny was gone. David picked up a spring from the Nanny-o-Meter™ and lovingly put it into his pocket.

Nathan had been about to grab that same piece, and he thought about screaming at David, but he didn't. Instead, Nathan just picked up a piece of dandruff Martin had left behind and put it in his own hair.

For dinner that night, Mrs. Wohlfardt tried to make a meat loaf shaped like Martin's head, and even though it looked oddly more like a mini hyena, the boys cried when they saw it. They refused to take a single bite.

CHAPTER
TWENTY-SIX

The next morning, the boys groggily slid out of bed at 7:55, didn't shower, and shuffled off to school just seconds before the first bell. They had become on-time, top students at school, but their string of successes came to an end with Martin's departure.

Once the boys had gone to school, the adult Wohlfardts went sadly to work. And that night, a brokenhearted Mrs. Wohlfardt began to iron Mr. Wohlfardt's tennis racket.

Weeping and desperate, Mrs. Wohlfardt made calls to find a new nanny. But she didn't find anyone that night, or over the many nights to come. There were few agencies with available nannies, and frankly, several of those who had someone to offer refused to offer them to the Wohlfardts.

"This is getting upsetting," said Mr. Wohlfardt, quite aware that the rhyme wasn't up to his usual high standards.

As time went on, the boys eventually fell into their old patterns. They started to bicker and fight. They turned their room into an awful mess. Their homework didn't come home, or if it did, it often went unworked. Their whole lives were going back to exactly what they'd been before Martin!

After about a month of Martinlessness, Mrs. Wohlfardt got on the phone one Friday night and, as luck would have it, she managed to book a new nanny on her very first call.

Early the next morning, while the boys were in bed, the winds blew and rattled the windows. The house shook. The boys jumped out of bed and ran to the window. Could it be? They even thought they saw a giant mustache swirling through the air, which actually could have been two identical long brown birds flying side by side.

Hurricane winds screeched and screamed. Thunder crashed and lightning forked. A torrential rain poured.

And as the chandeliers began to clash and shake, the doorbell rang.

Mrs. Wohlfardt opened the door and someone stepped inside.

"Good day, I'm here from the Myron Hyron Dyron Childcare Agency of Monaco," the boys heard a booming voice echo all the

way up the stairs, down the hallway, and into their room.

"Here," the booming voice continued. "I would like to present you with my letters of recommendation, for I feel, with all my heart, liver, kidneys, spleen, and left knee, that a quality childcare provider provides written letters of recommendation immediately upon

entering the home in which she, or in this case, he, will be nannyinginging."

After hearing that, David looked at Nathan. Nathan looked at David. And for the first time in weeks, they were both thinking the exact same thing:

Was the new nanny not really a *new* nanny at all?

Was it . . . Martin? Was he back?

There was only one way to find out. The boys stomped down the stairs to see who was there.

Nathan reached the bottom of the stairs first.

He stopped and gasped.

David was right behind him.

He, too, was so surprised that he fell off the last step. Then they tumbled onto the floor in a heap.

It sure looked like Martin Healey Discount, though this guy didn't have a mustache. But, as

David pointed out, Myron Hyron Dyron has the initials MHD!

"Hello, gents," the nanny said. "Are you perhaps interested at all in taking a ski trip?"

"You're hired!" said Nathan and David.

"Indeed you are!" said Mr. and Mrs. Wohlfardt.

"And Myron Hyron Dyron is a *wonderful*, rhyming name!" added Mr. Wohlfardt.

The parents—and their boys—were overjoyed at meeting this "new" nanny. Somehow they knew, they just knew, that things would be all right again in the Wohlfardt household.

It's possible that Nathan spoke for the whole family when he whispered to David, "I think we got the exact nanny we want!"

And David, without a moment of hesitation, whispered back, "I'll go order another spy detector kit."

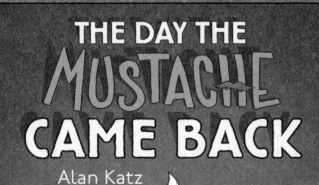

THE DAY THE MUSTACHE CAME BACK

Alan Katz

The new nanny at the front door said his name was Myron Hyron Dyron. But the way he looked, the way he spoke, even the way he smelled, told twin brothers Nathan and David Wohlfardt that the man standing before them was, in fact, their previous nanny, Martin Healey Discount.

"Martin! You're back!" exclaimed Nathan.

"Yes! You're back!" David said gleefully.

"What do you mean?" asked Myron.

"What do you mean, 'What do you mean?'?" asked David.

"What do you mean, 'What do you mean, what do you mean?'?" asked Myron.

"What do you mean, 'What do you mean, what do you mean, what do you mean?'?" asked Nathan.

"What I mean is my name is Myron. Myron Hyron Dyron. There is certainly no reason to address me as Martin."

"But you *are* Martin," David informed him. "Martin Healey Discount."

"Martin Healey Discount," Nathan added, "who was our nanny for about five months and twenty-nine days!"

"Actually, it was six months. Six months exactly, to the day," Myron said. "But as I said, that wasn't me."

"Oh, come on, Martin, give it up!" Nathan said. "We know it's you! Same face, same out-of-control mustache, same breath . . ."

"Yeah, plus Martin Healey Discount and Myron Hyron Dyron have the same initials.

You look the same, and . . . and . . . and . . . you knew how long Martin lived here before!" David said, as if reciting the charges against a wanted criminal. "So you are you!"

"I am indeed myself," Myron said. "But I am *not* Martin."

"Well, then, you must be twins!" David said.

"That's the first correct thing you've said," answered Myron. "Martin Healey Discount is my twin brother."

"*You're* a twin?" David gasped. "Just like us?"

"Well, not precisely like you," Myron told him. "For one thing, while the two of you live in the same house and are together constantly, such as in your room, at school, and on your recent ski trip, Martin and I have not actually seen each other for fourteen years, three months, and thirty-seven days."

Nathan and David didn't ask why he hadn't said that as fourteen years, four months, and seven days. Not because they weren't curious, but simply because they were both shocked that Myron knew about the ski trip the family had just taken. Also, it frankly never occurred to either one of them that there aren't any months with thirty-seven days.

"That's quite remarkable," Mrs. Wohlfardt said. "You are, in fact, the spitting image of Martin, Myron."

"Including the spit," David whispered to Nathan, having suddenly realized that he was soaked from the way Myron spit a little when he said words starting with *P* or *T* (just as Martin had always done).

"We knew Martin had five brothers and two sisters," Nathan said. "But we never knew he had a twin."

"Ah, I'm sure there are many things about Martin you don't know, little guy," Myron told him.

As a print and television writer, Alan Katz has majored in silliness for more than thirty years. He's written for a whole bunch of Emmy-nominated TV shows, animated series, award shows, and a slew of Nickelodeon projects. He is also the author of the Mustache series and many illustrated books of poems for kids, such as *Take Me Out of the Bathtub and Other Silly Dilly Songs*. He lives in Connecticut with his family, including his twin sons.

www.alankatzbooks.com

Kris Easler is the illustrator of the Mustache series. She has a master's degree in illustration from Savannah College of Art and Design and lives in Chicago, Illinois.

www.kriseasler.com